HOMEROOM HEADHUNTERS

Clay McLeod Chapman

Disney • Hyperion Books
New York

Text copyright © 2013 by Clay McLeod Chapman

All rights reserved. Published by Disney • Hyperion Books, an imprint of Disney Book Group. No part of this book may be reproduced or transmitted in any form or by any means, electronic or mechanical, including photocopying, recording, or by any information storage and retrieval system, without written permission from the publisher. For information address Disney • Hyperion Books, 125 West End Avenue, New York, New York 10023.

First Disney Hyperion paperback edition, 2014
1 3 5 7 9 10 8 6 4 2
J689-1817-1-14015
Printed in the United States of America
Library of Congress Catalog Control Number: 2012023957
ISBN 978-1-4231-5453-2

Visit www.DisneyBooks.com

SUSTAINABLE FORESTRY INITIATIVE

Certified Chain of Custody
Promoting Sustainable Forestry

www.sfiprogram.org
SFI-01054

The SFI label applies to the text stock

For Indrani Sen
Like a kid again

Part I: October

Just because you're paranoid doesn't mean they aren't after you. . . .
—Joseph Heller

THE BOY WHO CRIED FIRECRACKERS

Let's just get this out of the way up front:

I totally did not burn down my last school.

That's an overblown rumor. Whoever tells you I did is lying, straight to your face, so don't believe them.

It was only a couple of classrooms.

Most of the building is still standing.

And as far as the classrooms that *did* burn—well, that wasn't completely my fault either.

Honest.

And it wasn't like I planned to set my lab ablaze. It just kind of—well, you know.

It kinda just happened.

One day, you're learning about the digestive tract of amphibians, trying really, *really* hard to stay awake, when, out of nowhere, the fireworks stashed inside your backpack start shooting out from beneath your desk, and the hiss of mini-missiles sends everyone onto the floor like some middle-school Armageddon.

You know.

An accident.

In the spirit of total honesty, I'll admit, it wasn't completely out of nowhere.

The Bunsen burner probably had something to do with it.

Billy Templeton just had to drop a *double-dog dare* on me. If he hadn't goaded me into holding a bottle rocket over Mr. Bunsen's blue flame, that firecracker wouldn't have shot itself directly into my backpack, igniting the rest of my stash.

In my defense, just so you know, nobody got hurt.

Well. Mostly.

Do frogs count?

Who knew formaldehyde was that flammable? Just one stray spark from a Funky Monkey Fountain and—*KABOOM.*

Amphibious hand grenades. Wet shrapnel splattered against the blackboard, and tendrils of frog intestine tangled in Miss Beasley's hairdo.

She should have ducked.

I still maintain my innocence. You can't blame a kid for bringing his stash of firecrackers to school.

I mean, *you could.* But you shouldn't. Not in this case.

It was for a science project.

I swear.

I was working on a model of the big bang theory. And I needed—well, a big bang.

If you're going to talk about the cosmological conditions of the beginning of the universe, you need all the firepower you can find. That's just a scientific fact.

So, in a sense, this? *All this?* This was all in the name of science.

Okay. The truth—*the God's honest truth:* The morning this all happened, the people hereby designated as my parents decided to break some news to me.

I'll spare you the gore.

Let's just say it was the nonnegotiable, not-up-for-discussion-because-you're-young, just-take-it-all-in-and-let-it-fester kind of news.

The kind of news that makes your veins feel like one big wad of wicks, all of them tied to the firecracker you call your heart. Once your blood gets boiling, that fuse gets lit and there is just no extinguishing it. It's only a matter of time before— *KABLOOEY.* You're splashed all over the walls.

So. Just to set the record straight:

My name is Spencer Pendleton—and I totally did not set my last school on fire . . .

. . . On purpose.

All I wanted was for somebody to listen.

You believe me—right?

Right?

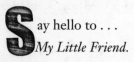

MY LITTLE FRIEND

S ay hello to . . .
My Little Friend.

My inhaler has gotten me out of more scraps with asthma than I can count.

Some kids have teddy bears. Others have blankies.

I cling to my inhaler like a third lung.

As far as medication goes, I've been on everything. *Twice.* Simply listing my prescriptions gets me wheezing. We've got long-acting beta-2 agonists, leukotriene modifiers, cromolyn, nedocromil, theophylline, ipratropium, fluticasone, budesonide, triamcinolone, flunisolide, beclomethasone, mometasone, salmeterol, formoterol, and zafirlukast. Even *pyromediakleptogrossulfate*!

That last one I made up just to see if you were still paying attention.

• • •

Monday. 7:54 a.m. Main hallway.

Welcome to the jungle.

The first bell at Greenfield Middle hadn't even rung yet and I already knew Riley Callahan. I had him pinned from the very moment we passed each other in the hall.

Riley has what the rest of us call Popular Guy Complexion.

I bet Riley Callahan has never had a blemish his entire life. Ten bucks says he's captain of the Pimple Cream Team.

Riley pressed his hand against my chest, his eyes locked onto My Little Friend dangling around my neck.

"Is that a PEZ dispenser?"

"It's an inhaler."

"You got asthma or something?"

"Nope," I said. "I just like inhaling corticosteroids for the fun of it."

"Watch your mouth . . . *newbie*. Before somebody knocks it off your face."

"Never heard of this Newbie guy before." I held out my hand. "Name's Spencer."

The muscles in Riley's jaw tensed, and everybody stopped walking. Bodies clotted up the hallway. The aroma of bloodlust filled the air, and, before I knew what was happening, I found myself in the center of a boxing ring made up of our classmates.

One kid started chanting: "Fight! Fight! Fight!"

Then another: "Fight! Fight! Fight!"

Then three more, ten more, *twenty*, until the whole hallway was echoing: "FIGHT! FIGHT! FIGHT!"

Once the Ring of Death wraps around two students, only one is allowed to leave on his own two feet. That—or a teacher comes and breaks it up.

Everybody was waiting to see what Riley would do next.

I must admit, I was pretty curious myself.

I watched as the fingers on his right hand slowly curled up.

Uh-oh.

He reeled back his hand.

Not good, Spence. Not good at all.

Press the PAUSE button, please.

• • •

Flashback to a wise old woman saying: *Don't rock the boat.*

Mom had dropped me off at school that morning. She planted a kiss flat on my forehead in front of all the kids entering the building, even though I pleaded with her not to.

"Ready for your first day, hon?"

"Ready as I'll ever be."

"Did you remember to pack your inhaler?"

"Right here, Mom. . . ."

"Okay, then," she sighed. "Promise me one thing?"

". . . What's that?"

"Don't rock the boat, Spencer."

These were her words of wisdom.

Thanks a lot, Mom. . . .

• • •

Now press PLAY.

There I was, about to get my lights punched out, wondering if a fistfight with Riley Callahan constituted boat-rocking or not.

If it didn't, what I did next surely did:

I brought My Little Friend up to Riley's face and squeezed a long-winded spritz of chest steroids straight into his face. He clutched his eyes, yelling—then charged.

I stepped to my left, clearing a path directly into the lockers behind me. Riley's forehead met metal—*THWONK!*—sprawling him flat across the hallway floor.

Suddenly I was the captain of the USS *Saving My Ass*, navigating my way through a sea of students, setting sail for neutral waters.

How's that for boat-rocking?

I don't think I'd ever hauled my rear end that fast in my entire life.

That's when my lungs started to flutter.

Here it comes—I could feel it in my chest.

Little Friend, don't fail me now!

I brought my inhaler up to my mouth, squeezed . . .

. . . And nothing.

Empty.

I'd used up my medication on Riley's face.

This was bad. This was *really* bad.

A wave of light-headedness washed through my skull. My knees softened, sending me toppling onto the floor. I lay there on my back, face up, staring at the ceiling. Prickles of light popped up at the bottom of my eyeballs.

Then things got mondo bizarro.

One of the fiberglass panels along the ceiling pulled itself back, and I saw a hand. A pale hand. *A girl's hand*—reaching out from inside the ceiling.

The hand was holding an inhaler.

Oxygenated blood must've stopped flowing to my head because clearly I was hallucinating.

Angels. The heavens opening. That sort of thing.

Totally delusional.

That hand dropped the inhaler onto my chest, and I grabbed it just in time to squeeze off a gust of medicated air. Oxygen eased into my lungs again.

Hallelujah, I thought. I'm not dying today!

All thanks to a guardian angel hidden behind the ceiling panels.

Kids stopped walking through the hallway and circled around me on the floor. All I could see were their curious faces staring down.

Mr. Jim Pritchard, my new assistant principal, rushed through the hall and kneeled next to me. "Are you okay? Can you breathe?"

"Think so," I huffed.

"What happened?"

"An angel reached down from heaven and gave me an inhaler. . . ."

I pointed toward the ceiling—but the panel was in place, like nothing had happened.

I glanced at the inhaler in my hand, looking for the name on the prescription.

Winston Reynolds.

I read the date along the side. Expired. Five years before.

I'd just sucked down moldy-oldie medication.

No wonder I was seeing things.

"I'm taking you to the clinic." The skepticism was thick in Mr. Pritchard's voice. "Get you checked for a concussion."

I had the sneaking feeling he didn't believe in angels.

THE GIRL ON THE TELEPHONE POLE

first saw her at the corner of Spring Street and Weeping Willow.

I had missed my bus. That meant I was hoofing it home.

Great.

As far as first days go, this one couldn't have gotten much worse. All I wanted to do now was keep walking until I reached the ocean. Or the edge of the world.

Or my old house.

Who would notice if I was gone?

I was only a few blocks away from school when, out of the corner of my eye, I could have sworn I saw somebody staring at me.

I pivoted and came face-to-face with a phantom photocopy: Runny ink cheeks. Fuzzy button nose. Dark eyes. Bad weather had blurred her features.

Big bold capital letters, lined up along her chin, read:

MISSING.

Below that, in smaller print, her name:

Sully Tulliver.

It was a yearbook picture. I could tell from the pose. The half smile. Didn't think much of it until I bumped into her again at the corner of Tompkins and Remar.

Her eyes seemed to be watching me.

I wondered what color they were.

She must've been about my age. Maybe a little older. Sort of cute.

Who was she?

She was waiting for me at Apricot Avenue and Bougainvillea.

And again at Spruce and Veranda Avenue.

Wherever I went, there she was, staring right back at me.

"What're you looking at?"

I almost expected her to answer. But she just watched me as I wandered off.

I started making up a backstory for her on my walk home. By the time I made it to my block, I had her entire life mapped out:

Sully Tulliver ran away from home because nobody believed her when she said she'd seen a hand reach out from her new school's ceiling. Imagine a Lady of the Lake moment, with King Arthur clamoring for Excalibur—only this time, instead of a sword, it's an inhaler. The kids at school thought Sully was off her rocker, making the whole thing up for attention.

I would've believed her.

Wherever you are, Sully—I sure hope it's better than here.

I pulled one of her MISSING flyers off a telephone pole and folded it to fit into my back pocket, like she'd written me a note or something.

At home, I pinned it to my bedroom wall.

She looked pixelated. There had to be thousands. Tens of thousands. Maybe even a million little photocopied dots coming together to form her face, making up her eyebrows, her cheeks, the bridge of her nose.

The dots formed her eyes like a constellation of stars surrounding two black planets.

There's Andromeda. There's Orion.

And there's Sully.

Looking into that vast galaxy of Sully Tulliver's MISSING flyer, I ended up getting lost in the pixels. I spent the whole afternoon counting them, losing my place, and starting all over again.

"Ready for dinner, hon?" Mom asked, peeking her head into my bedroom. "Who's that?"

"Nobody." I caught myself just before I said: *A friend.*

TALL TALES
AT THE
DINNER TABLE

My mom makes meat loaf sandwiches when she wants something from me.

Here's her technique:

1. Make me my favorite meal.
2. Wait until my mouth's full of meat loaf.
3. Force me to do her bidding.

From the moment I smelled steaming ground beef in the oven, I knew something was up. Sure enough, Mom ambushed me in the kitchen with a plate of her mind-controlling meat loaf.

"Surprise!" She blew a tuft of chestnut hair out of her face.

"To what do I owe the honor?" I asked.

"To celebrate your first day at your new school. I want to hear all about it."

"Not much to tell, really. . . ."

"Come on—I made your favorite." Mom smiled. *"Meeeeat-loaf sand-weeech-es."*

"With cornflakes crumbled on top?"

"Yep."

"And barbecue sauce?"

"Yep."

"And no green peppers?"

"Notta one."

Honey-glazed carrots glistened under the kitchen light like candy. I could feel my tummy surrendering to my mom already.

Keep cool. Savor my meal. Remain fully aware of the fact that Mom will drop one of her let's-make-a-deal bombs at any moment.

She held off until my first bite.

"So . . . are you gonna tell me how school was, or do I have to guess?"

"Sucked," I said.

"Sucked?"

"Sucked."

"How so?"

"Just sucked."

"Any particular reason?"

"A million reasons."

"Tell me." She genuinely looked concerned.

"We'll be sitting here all night. . . ."

"I've got the time."

"Your sandwich is gonna get cold."

"I can eat and listen."

"*My* sandwich's gonna get cold."

"You can eat and talk."

"You told me not to talk with my mouth full."

"You know what I mean."

My second bite of meat loaf was so downright delectable I nearly lost my train of thought.

"Okay," I said, chewing. A solid stalling technique here for all you future stallers out there: *Chew each mouthful fifty times before swallowing.*

Works every time.

"Well?"

"Okay." I swallowed. "First thing that happened, right when I first walked into the building, before the first bell even rang. . . ."

Big sip of milk. A third bite of my meat loaf sandwich.

Tenth chew, eleventh chew, twelfth chew, thirteenth . . .

"Any day now, Spence. . . ." Mom was beginning to lose her patience.

"Okay, okay." I swallowed. "I had to break up this fight with a few eighth graders."

"Eighth graders . . . and you? Really?"

"Three of them." I nodded. "They were going to town on this defenseless sixth grader. . . ."

"And, pray tell, what was your involvement in all of this?"

"I did what any civic-minded citizen would do. I got right in their face and said, *Pick on somebody in your own grade!*"

"Please tell me you didn't, Spencer. *Please.*"

"I had to, Mom. . . . They all had penny rolls in their hands."

". . . Penny rolls?"

"They're like brass knuckles for middle schoolers. You hold them inside your fist for extra punch."

"How do you even know about these things?"

"Middle school isn't what it used to be, Mom. It might've been all peace, love, and understanding when you were in the seventh grade, but now it's more like tribal warfare."

"Sounds like it."

"So one of them pulls back his hand, ready to clobber me." I reeled my own hand back for dramatic effect. "But I duck just in time. His penny-fisted punch lands straight in the assistant principal's face!"

"Wait." Mom blinked. "*Assistant principal?* Where'd he come from?"

"That's what I'm trying to tell you!"

"Sorry, sorry."

"He'd come in to break it up—and BAM! Fifty cents right in the nose."

Mom was staring at me like I had meat loaf all over my face.

". . . What?" I asked.

"You didn't have an asthma attack, did you? Because this sounds a lot like a *Spencer had another asthma attack and is covering it up with a whopper* kind of story."

"Just a little one . . ."

Mom took in a quick breath, holding it. "You had your inhaler, right?"

I tugged the shoestring from around my neck with my thumb, pulling My Little Friend out from underneath my T-shirt.

"Good." She released the air in her lungs. "You're supposed to call me if you have an attack, remember? *Always*. You promised."

"It wasn't a big deal."

Mom pressed her palm against the side of her head and stared at me. She suddenly looked exhausted.

"You know," she said, "it wouldn't be such a bad idea to tell me what *really* happened at school today."

"What's that supposed to mean?"

"Ever hear the story about the boy who cried wolf?"

"You don't believe me."

She held up her hands. "I just wonder if you'd have an easier time fitting in if you, you know, *told the truth now and then*."

Now it was my turn not to say anything for a while.

"Dad would've believed me," I said finally.

"*Spencer.* I didn't say I didn't believe you. . . ."

"Dad would've thought I'd done the right thing."

"Well—your father's not here, is he?"

Stalemate. There was nothing left for us to do but stare each other down.

I caved in first. "Who says I want to fit in, anyway?"

"Don't you?"

"Not really."

"Why not?"

"What's the point of being just like everybody else?"

"Seems like it'd be easier to make friends if you didn't push people away all the time."

"I'm making plenty of friends already."

"Like who?"

"Like Sully."

"Sully?"

Whoops.

"Just some girl." I shrugged. "She followed me around all day today."

"Tell you what." Mom paused for dramatic effect. "I'll make a deal with you. . . ."

Didn't I tell you?

"Promise me you'll keep an open mind and stay out of trouble," she said. "And I'll make meat loaf sandwiches once a week."

I mulled it over. "I'll give you six months."

"Only six months?"

"A trial period."

"At least promise me you'll be on your best behavior," she said. "Can you do that much?"

"Fine. I'll try."

My plate was clean. Mom had barely touched her meat loaf sandwich.

"You gonna eat that?" I asked.

"All yours."

KEEPER OF THE GRAFFITI

 word of advice to all the newbies out there: *Never head to the boys' room alone.*

I should've known better. Between classes on my second day, I stumbled upon Riley Callahan and a couple of his Cro-Magnon cronies sneaking a cigarette in the middle stall.

"What are you doing in here?" Riley flicked his cancer stick into the toilet.

"I was just leaving. . . ."

I spun 180 degrees, but it was too late. I found myself flanked by two eighth graders. They flossed their arms through mine and carried me kicking into the middle stall—where Riley was waiting, toilet seat up and everything.

How considerate.

"We've got to stop meeting like this, Riley. . . ."

"Shut it," he said. A red welt had blossomed across his

forehead from his run-in with the locker. His eyes were swollen from my inhaler hose-down. Each socket was wrapped in a pink ring, like he was suffering from a nasty case of cotton-candy conjunctivitis. "I don't care how tough you think you were at your last school; maggots start at the bottom of the food chain."

"I'll make a note of it, thanks."

Next thing you know, I was completely inverted, literally head over heels above the bowl. The change in my pocket was falling out, landing in the water with a series of loud *kerplunk*s.

Kerplunk, kerplunk, kerplunk!

"Make a wish," Riley said, flushing.

You better believe I made a wish. It was something along the lines of, *Please oh please oh please get me out of here.* . . .

"How long do you think you can hold your breath?"

"Not long enough."

"Too bad," he said. "I bet a blast from your inhaler would come in pretty handy right about now. . . ."

All I could do was breathe in deep and close my eyes before the whirlpool sucked my head in.

Riley's cronies gave me a few moments underwater to reflect on how life at Greenfield had been going thus far for me.

Let's see: Day one—asthma attack. Day two—head flushed down toilet.

Only 178 school days left to go.

"Better find your spot on the totem pole fast," Riley called out from above the water's surface, "or some friends who'll watch your back."

When I washed ashore, I found myself alone, stranded on my own tiny toilet bowl island.

A bathroom-bound Robinson Crusoe.

I sat there listening to the sound of water dribbling off my clothes.

Blip.

Blip.

Blip.

"Mr. Simms." Assistant Principal Pritchard's voice crackled from the intercom above my head. "Come to the boys' locker room. We have a busted pipe. Busted pipe in the locker room . . ."

That's when it caught my eye. Some peculiar bathroom-stall graffiti.

A stick figure. Holding a spear.

Just above its head, somebody had written:

WE ARE WATCHING YOU.

If there's one thing I've discovered, no matter what academic institution I've transferred to, it's that you can learn all you need to know about a school by its graffiti.

If you want to find out what's *really* going on within the hallowed halls of your school, don't crack open the yearbook. Sneak into the rear stall of the boys' bathroom and read up.

This is where the real history is written.

Who kissed who. Who used to like who.

The graffiti here sucked. That was just a sad fact. A finger painting from a kindergarten class would have been better than what was thrown up on the walls here.

So I fished a Sharpie out from my soaked shorts, then peeked through the stall door.

All clear.

I found a free space and started. I didn't have a lot of time before the bell rang, but more than enough to sprawl my masterpiece above the toilet paper dispenser:

A portrait of our own beloved Riley hunched over in *The Thinker* pose, deep in contemplation, with his shorts down at his ankles.

I am the Van Gogh of vandalism.

Suddenly I heard a shuffle from the neighboring stall.

I leaned over and peered under the stall partition.

There, in plain view, I saw a pair of bare feet.

Someone's in the bathroom with me. Right in the next stall. A second ago it was empty. . . . And what's up with the missing shoes?

"Hello?"

The feet disappeared.

". . . Hello?"

Silence.

"Who's there?"

Okay. Keep calm. Whoever it is, they're probably just as scared as I am.

Play it cool, play it cool and—

I rushed out of my stall and kicked open the neighboring door.

"Gotcha!"

Empty. I threw open the other stall doors to see if whoever it was had slipped into a different toilet.

Nobody. I was completely alone.

The bell for class rang. I looked down and noticed ink smudges on my hands. *Great.* I beelined for the sink. A good way to get caught throwing up graffiti is to have black Magic Marker all over your fingers.

The ink wasn't coming off. I kept scrubbing, until I saw something behind my reflection. Above the row of stalls.

Turning around, I looked up at the ceiling as a fiberglass panel slipped back.

"You've got to be kidding me. . . ."

ORAL
REPORTS

Something very strange was going on here.

Somebody was screwing with me.

But before I could do anything about it I had to suffer through second period.

I had Scotch-taped one of Sully Tulliver's MISSING flyers to the inside of my three-ring binder. That way she'd stick with me through all six periods.

"Any bright ideas on how to survive the next fifty-eight minutes?" I asked the picture.

I could almost hear Sully answer: *Set your desk on fire?*

"I've got a better plan. . . ."

I took a seat at the very back of the room and assembled my sharpest pencils.

"Today, we spearfish for medium-textured, fine-fissured fiberglass ceiling panels. . . ."

Thar she blows!

My record from my old school was six pencils in thirty minutes—and on day two here at Greenfield, I planned on obliterating my top score, in world history class.

"Wish me luck," I whispered to Sully's picture.

"Can I get everybody's attention, please?" Mrs. Witherspoon called out just as the bell rang. "Time for our oral presentations."

My chest seized. Oral—*what*? My mind drew a blank.

"*Two minutes,*" she said. "Topic of your choice. Now, who'd like to go first?"

Witherspoon wouldn't pick me. Not on my second day. Not with only one day to prepare. That would be too cruel. No teacher is that—

"*Mr. Pendleton.*" Mrs. Witherspoon zeroed in on me, a hunter eyeing her quarry. "Might I ask what all the pencils are for?"

"You can never be too prepared, ma'am."

"Maybe you'd like to start us off, then?" Mrs. Witherspoon suggested. "What better way for you and the class to get acquainted."

Everybody's heads turned. No one looked all too happy to be making my acquaintance.

Where did this pack of rabid werekids come from? It was like they could sniff the fresh-student smell on me and were ready to pounce.

"Is it possible to take a rain check?"

"Just because you're new to our school doesn't mean you

can come unprepared to my class, Mr. Pendleton. What sort of example would that set?"

Was that . . . a challenge? I do believe so.

Greenfield really hadn't rolled out the red carpet for me. First, Riley sent me toilet diving. My clothes were still damp. And now Mrs. Wither*whatever* had to throw down the gauntlet.

I had tried to play nice—but she'd clearly provoked me.

I'd suffered enough indignities.

Time for payback.

"Well, I guess when you put it that way . . . *I'd love to.*"

"I have my stopwatch ready to go whenever you are."

I took my time walking up to the front of the class, sensing each and every eye on me. My classmates' stares practically pinned my limbs to the blackboard like a frog about to get dissected.

Not one of them knew what to make of me.

Or cared.

Here's a bit of advice for the newbies, courtesy of yours truly: *The best defense is a good offense.*

Looking around the room, I could tell I wouldn't be making any BFFs here. If I was going to crash and burn, I might as well have some fun with it.

"I recently moved here from . . ."

I scanned over the maps of the world wallpapering the classroom, thinking of a million and one other places I'd rather be.

". . . Papa New Guinea," I said.

"Don't you mean Pa*pua* New Guinea?" Mrs. Witherspittoon

asked. "The islands in the southwestern Pacific Ocean?"

"That's what I said," I said, as if I actually knew what I was saying. "Didn't I just say that? Have *you* ever been to Papua New Guinea before, Mrs. Witherspork?"

"Spoon," she corrected me. "It's Wither*spoon*."

"Well—*have you?*"

"No, I have not."

"Well, then," I said. "Maybe you might learn a little something today!"

A jaw dropped in the third row.

"Everybody in my family is an anthropologist," I began. "I'm actually thinking about continuing their research on the Swanahanzi tribe located there."

"The—*who?*" Witherspank asked, eyes widening.

"Swanahanzi. Headhunters. Not the nicest neighbors. . . ."

This was good. This was really good.

"Sounds . . . dangerous," a flawlessly coiffed blonde uttered from the front row. She was wearing a tennis outfit.

Does this school even have a tennis team?

"It most certainly is," I agreed, before turning back to Mrs. Whitherspazz. "Did you know that the Swanahanzi are the only known tribe that continues to practice headhunting?"

". . . No, I didn't."

"You mean to tell me—*and the class*—that you've never heard one bit of information, *not one tiny iota of detail*, about the Swanahanzi tribe? *Ever?*"

"I guess not."

"The Swanahanzi build huts made out of human bones and—"

"I'm not sure if this is the most appropriate topic," Mrs. Witherspelunking started to interrupt.

But there was no stopping me.

I cut her off. "When a tribesman kills an enemy, they'll bring the body back to their village and remove the head. Then they sew the eyes and lips shut, and eat the brains from the skull like it's a bowl. . . ."

"Spencer—"

"They'll add a squirt of eyeball jam for flavor and slurp the whole thing down, believing they absorb the essence of their enemy. . . ."

"Spencer, please—"

"And it's been rumored," I said, gearing up for the cherry on top, "that members of the Swanahanzi have found their way to the United States, perhaps to this very town—*so you better watch out!*"

"SPENCER!"

Suddenly those rabid werekids looked like a herd of bewildered deer caught in the headlights.

Silence. Sweet, baffled silence.

Spence: *One*.

Witherspoilsport's world history class: *Zero*.

"Well . . . what a vivid imagination you have, Mr. Pendleton."

She gave a less-than-enthusiastic golf clap.

"Who knows?" I couldn't resist. "They may even be here, in school, hunting as we speak!"

Your two minutes are up, Spencer!

I could feel every eye follow me as I strutted back to my desk.

How was that for a first-impression preemptive strike?

"So," Mrs. Witherspittle sighed, "who'd like to go next? Anybody?"

The girl in the tennis getup impaled the air with her arm.

"Sarah. The class is all yours."

The tennis pro cleared her throat as she made her way to the front. "Good morning, class. My name is Sarah Haversand—and today, I'd like to talk about school spirit."

Oh boy. Here we go. . . .

"School spirit is a vital part of any school. It is the very life-blood of our student body."

"Mr. Simms." Assistant Principal Pritchard's voice blurted out from the intercom over Sarah's head, interrupting her presentation. "We have a busted pipe in the boys' bathroom. Busted pipe in the boys' bathroom. . . ."

Where were we?

Ah, yes! Back to spearfishing medium-textured, fine-fissured fiberglass ceiling tiles.

I waited until Mrs. Withersplat's back was turned, before hurling my first pencil straight up at the ceiling.

Bull's-eye!

First throw was a success. Right into the blubbery underbelly of white fiberglass. The pencil was a little crooked, like an upside-down Leaning Tower of Pisa, but it would do.

"I feel as if the students here at Greenfield don't have enough school spirit," Sarah continued. "While I, for one, sometimes feel like I have way too much."

Throw number two was an utter dud. Not enough thrust.

If I was going to break my record, I needed to start some rapid-fire harpooning—*and fast*.

I steadied my arm for the next shot.

Deep breath.

Focus.

Aim.

And—*fire!*

I threw that pencil harder than any javelin. Its sharpened end buried itself all the way through the panel. This was Olympic gold medal material.

Then I heard a grunt above my head.

I rolled my eyes up while keeping my head bowed.

There.

One of the panels in the ceiling seemed to *breathe*. The fiber-glass bulged just a bit before settling back.

"When we come together and share our pride at pep rallies," Sarah proclaimed, "Greenfield becomes more than just another school. It feels like we're a family."

Then it happened.

The panel directly above my head pulled back, leaving an inch of darkness.

And then—I totally saw eyes. They were staring right at me.

Somebody was up there!

I bolted up from my chair, pointing toward the panel.

"Look! Look!"

"What are you doing, Spencer?" Mrs. Witherspinster stormed over, ready to throttle me in front of the entire class.

"The ceiling! Somebody's up there!"

At that very moment, my Leaning Pencil of Pisa decided to loosen itself from the ceiling panel and hit my world history teacher directly in her left eye.

THE ASS
IN ASSISTANT
PRINCIPAL

You'd believe me if I told you that I didn't staple Assistant Principal Pritchard's hand on purpose, right?

Obviously I had been aiming for the hand reaching out from his ceiling.

Pritchard grabbed me when he should've been helping me go after *whoever* it was creeping through the crawl space of his school. I even had to jump *on top* of Pritchard's desk so I could reach the fiberglass panel that had just opened *above* his head.

Not that Pritchard noticed that part. All he saw was me—this lunatic seventh grader pouncing on top of his desk, grabbing his stapler, flipping it open like a butterfly knife, and trying to make a break for the rooftop.

A stapler isn't the best choice of weaponry, I know, but I had to think on the fly. So I snatched the first thing I could get my hands on.

If Pritchard hadn't wrapped his arms around my stomach and tried to pull me down, I wouldn't have lost my balance and slapped his stapler against his wrist.

But I'm getting way ahead of myself.

• • •

"Do you really expect us to believe you saw someone in the ceiling?" Withersprout huffed. Her eye was looking a bit blood-shot from where the pencil had hit it.

Thank goodness it had been the eraser end.

"I was trying to flush them out!"

So that part was a lie. But the first part wasn't.

Honest.

"There's no one up there!"

"Mrs. Witherspoon." Assistant Principal Pritchard calmly cleared his throat. "Did you leave the rest of your class unattended?"

Witherspore's face flushed, matching the red hue of her pencil injury.

"I should get back. . . ."

"Thank you," Pritchard said. "I'll handle this from here."

Witherspleen gave me the stink eye with her wounded peeper as she left. Pritchard waited until the door had completely closed behind her, sealing the two of us inside his office.

"Any idea why you're here, Mr. Pendleton?"

"Almost gouging my history teacher's eye out with a pencil?"

"Can you think of any other reason why?"

"You got me." I shrugged.

"No guess whatsoever?"

I made a personal inventory of all the things I'd done since arriving at Greenfield two days ago, trying to figure out what I was getting pinned for: Pepper-spraying another student with my inhaler? Tagging the bathroom stall with a permanent marker?

Possibly.

I can neither confirm nor deny any of these accusations. Until I know what exactly I'm being tried for, I am pleading the Fifth.

"I'm not out to get you," he said. "I'm merely here for the truth."

"Sure hope you find it, sir. . . ."

When Pritchard leaned back in his chair, I caught the slightest smirk creeping out from the corner of his lips.

Did I just make him laugh? I think I did!

He tried to swallow his chuckle by covering it with a cough, but I totally heard it.

"You know, Spencer—you remind me a lot of myself when I was your age. Smart kid. Quick with a comeback. Chip on your shoulder."

Touché, Pritchard. Nice touch. Butter me up all you want, but I won't fold that easily.

"How'd that work out for you?" I asked.

"Not so well."

Can I trust him? Tell him what I saw in Witherwhatev's class?

"Adjusting to a new school can be difficult," he said. "I understand that."

"You do?"

"There's a whole new set of rules to learn, and that can be tough," he said. "Now—I went ahead and did a little homework on you."

"You did my homework—*for me?*"

"No. I did my homework *on* you."

"It wasn't my fault, sir . . . whatever it was."

"I want you to know that I'm willing to give you the benefit of the doubt here, Spencer. As far as coming to my school is concerned, you have a clean slate."

"That's a relief to hear."

"All I ask for in return, however—is a promise."

"What kind of promise?"

Assistant Principal Pritchard leaned in closer. "How about we make a deal?"

What is it with adults trying to make deals with me?

"Well, Jim," I leaned in. "Do you mind if I call you Jim?"

"Let's stick with Principal for now."

"Guess we'll just have to work our way up to Jim," I said, chuckling.

"It's Principal Pritchard."

"Don't you mean *Ass*-istant Principal, sir?"

"Mr. Pritchard is fine."

"You see, *Ass*-istant Principal Pritchard, sir—well, it's complicated."

Pause. Total silence. Staring contest.

Pritchard cleared his throat. "I put in a phone call to the *ass*-istant principal at your last school."

". . . You did?"

"I've heard pretty much all I need to hear from Mrs. Condrey about how you handled yourself there. . . . But I'd rather hear it from you."

I looked at the clock. If I really milked it, I could stay in his office until second period ended.

"Well," I said. "Where would you like me to begin?"

That's when the panel above Pritchard's head pulled back a crack.

Somebody was up there.

I'm being spied on.

Pritchard hadn't noticed. He was too busy talking about I don't know what.

"We discovered a lot of items have mysteriously gone missing this morning," he continued. "Office supplies, mainly. You wouldn't know anything about this, would you?"

This was my chance.

If Pritchard was ever going to believe me about somebody lurking in his ceiling, I'd need proof. I needed to take action.

Play it cool. Don't look up.

Then I noticed the stapler.

On the count of three—jump on the desk, grab the stapler, slip through the ceiling, and . . .

Not my best thought-out plan, I know. But we were at war with an invisible enemy—and as a man of action, it was time to show this phantom offender who it was dealing with!

One: I took a deep breath.

Two: I slid to the edge of my seat.

Three: I pounced.

And . . . ? Well, you know the rest.

THE GIRL
ON THE
MILK CARTON

You want gravy with that?" A loose lock of gray spilled from the cafeteria lady's hairnet. "Don't take it unless you're gonna eat it."

"Are we in the middle of a famine or something?"

"We got a cafeteria bandit on our hands again. Somebody's always snitching food, no different this year."

Why anyone would pilfer potatoes and gravy from the lunch ladies was beyond me.

Making my way through the cafeteria with my tray, I could hear the faint snarls of whispering werekids behind my back:

"That's him! That's the newbie. . . ."

"Did you hear? He just attacked the assistant principal. . . ."

"What a freak. . . ."

I conjured up another conversation with Sully:

SULLY: *So—how's the whole loner thing working out for you, Spence?*

ME: *Not that good, to be completely honest. Nobody's going to believe me about what I saw in Mrs. Withersponge's class—or in the hall.*

SULLY: *Maybe you should lay off the smart-aleck shtick for a bit, see if that helps.*

ME: *And ruin the amazing reputation I'm making for myself? Never. . . .*

"Mr. Simms." Assistant Principal Pritchard's voice sputtered out over the intercom. "Please come to Mrs. Witherspoon's class. We have a busted pipe. Busted pipe in Mrs. Witherspoon's classroom. . . ."

I shuffled to the nearest empty seat and took it. All I wanted was to eat in peace.

"Wrong table, *Spazzma.* . . ."

Turns out I had landed at Riley Callahan's table. He and his cloned Cro-Magnon cronies waltzed up with their lunches, looking none too happy about my company.

"You've got ten seconds to find another place to eat," he said. "Or we escort you to another table by your tongue."

"Look—I'm sorry for macing you in the face with my inhaler yesterday, okay?"

"Ten."

"Can we start over again? Clean slate?"

"Nine."

"I'm really not that bad of a guy once you get to know me. . . ."

"Eight."

"Please." I took a quick swig of my milk. "All I want is to eat my lunch and—"

I choked. Milk flooded out of my nostrils.

There, staring at me from the back of my milk carton—was her.

Not just any her.

Her.

Sully. *Sully Tulliver* was on my milk carton. Same black-and-white yearbook picture.

"Who's that?" Riley leaned forward.

I covered the carton with my hand before he could get a good look at the picture. "Nobody."

Riley guffawed. "That your girlfriend or something?"

"She's not my girlfriend."

"Check it out!" Riley laughed as he brought his sandwich up for a bite. "Spazzma found himself a girlfriend on the back of his milk carton!"

Beaming at his own putdown, Riley took a toothy chomp out of his sandwich and . . .

SNAP!

Both slices of bread disintegrated into crumbs, and the crusts fell away from his fingers. Riley's eyes grew into gulfs of panic as they stared down at the spring-loaded bar pinching his lower lip.

"Be careful." I reached for the dangling mouse trap. "Don't touch it. . . ."

Riley slapped my hands away, whimpering like a puppy. The skin around his lip was quickly turning a deep purple. He scooted backward and off his seat, nearly falling to the floor.

Automatically, I peered up. The panel above our table was pulled back.

"Look!" I yelled. "Everybody—look up!"

Everyone's eyes remained on me.

Skeptical eyes.

"We're not alone! Don't you see? There are people in the ceiling! In the walls! *They're everywhere!*"

A panel over the next table pulled itself back.

I needed to act fast if I was going to get people to believe me. To see what I saw.

But how?

Looking down, I noticed the perfectly round mound of processed potatoes on my tray.

Mashed potatoes. The most perfect weapon of mass consumption ever:

A. Slightly larger than a tennis ball, perfect for the palm of your hand.

B. Soft but not mushy, and thick enough to retain structural integrity.

C. Has an outer layer of gravy, perfect for a spitball pitch.

D. When it hits its target—and it most definitely always hits its target—that round mound of gravy-layered softness explodes into a paste of creamy napalm.

I stood on top of my table and threw a handful of mashed potatoes at the open space in the ceiling.

"Take that!"

I swear I had been aiming for the ceiling.

The mushy missile was well on its way to hitting its intended target, arcing up toward the shifting ceiling tiles, only to lose its momentum somewhere along the way and begin a descent back to the ground.

In retrospect, I can see how it might've looked like I was actually pitching my potatoes into the face of Sarah Haversand, who was sitting three tables over.

Sarah was merely the victim of food-fight friendly fire.

Cafeteria collateral damage.

As soon as her tennis whites disappeared beneath a splatter pattern of mushy spuds, she started screaming, while Riley—mousetrap still dangling from his lower lip—took this opportunity to pick up his lunch tray and swing it at my kneecaps.

Still standing on top of our table, I leapt.

A quick description of our lunch tables, or "mobile stool units," as they are called in the cafeteria equipment catalogue: each rectangular table has a hinge in the middle, allowing for easy storage. The flat plastic seats are mounted along the sides. If there aren't enough people weighing the table down to the floor, and an improper balance of mass is suddenly placed on one end, the entire table can spring closed on itself—like a reverse bear trap.

When I came careering down, landing at the edge of our lunch table—the impact sent the unit bending upward, instantly turning itself into a spring-loaded catapult.

Whatever food had been on our table was slung in all directions.

For the people sitting to our right, a tidal wave of gravy washed over them.

For the people sitting to our left, a face full of cafeteria shrapnel: potatoes, green beans, carrot sticks, pizza slices, bologna.

You name it. Completely battered, smothered, and covered.

And it was looking like it was all my fault.

Again.

In the dawn of every seventh grader's life, there comes a point where he must decide:

To food-fight—or not to food-fight?

That, my friends, was the question.

And since I was already in detention, the answer was obvious.

Leaping to my feet, I gave the battle cry:

"FOOOOOOD FIGHT!"

A blur of edible mortar shells flew through the air as each student lobbed his or her own projectile of mashed potatoes.

Clothes were covered.

Walls were splattered.

Gravy dripped.

For a few glorious seconds, it looked like it was snowing inside the cafeteria.

This was going to get me into history books:

Spence Pendleton. Food revolutionary.

Cafeteria freedom fighter.

OVERDUE
BOOKS

Dried mashed potato doesn't come out of your clothes all that easily.

Or your hair. Or your textbooks.

Or anything else.

Surprise.

The goo congealed *fast*, crusting into a white shell, encasing everything it came into contact with.

That included around seventy werekids, and they all wanted to see me strung up from one of the gym's basketball nets.

So the food fight might've been a bad idea.

And I was only halfway through my second day at Greenfield.

Instead of letting those stained students out of school early—as I had suggested, to wash up and slip into something clean—Assistant Principal Pritchard made us change into gym uniforms. Everybody who had taken part in the infamous Mashed Potato Middle School Massacre was now sporting red short shorts and gray tees with GREENFIELD emblazoned across the chest.

Very fashionable.

•••

The cafeteria itself was covered. The ceiling had potato icicles dangling down. There was even a mashed potato snow angel from where some poor kid must have slipped and fell, then fanned his or her arms and legs over the floor.

Now it was cleanup time, and guess who got volunteered?

"Sure made a mess of this place, didn't you?"

Mr. Simms was the janitor at Greenfield. He took one look at the crusty chaos covering the cafeteria and shook his head.

"I didn't mean for it to get this messy," I said. "I swear I'll clean it all up."

"If you tried cleaning this by yourself," he chuckled, "you'd be here till Christmas. And from the looks of it—*it's already snowed!*"

Mr. Simms slapped his hip so hard, all the keys on the retractable chain attached to his belt jangled. As long as he was laughing, I figured I wasn't in such big trouble.

"I've never seen so many confused students in my life," he wheezed, then bent over, placing his hands on his knees. His lungs had a wet sound to them.

Sounded like an asthma attack.

I pulled the string with My Little Friend over my head.

"Here," I said. "Take a puff of this."

Mr. Simms took a quick hit, and his breathing eased back to normal.

"Much obliged."

"I'm really sorry, Mr. Simms," I said. And I was. Wasn't his fault, you know? Janitors get dumped on by just about everybody here; the last thing I wanted was to pile on.

"Don't worry about it." Mr. Simms plopped his mop onto the floor. "Let's get cleaning."

Thirty-two tables. All covered in white scabs.

First I tried wetting down the dried potatoes, but that just turned the gunk into a messy paste. Mr. Simms handed me a putty knife and advised me to scrape the potato away like it was old paint.

"We'll be done in no time," he said.

"I'll have graduated from college before we're finished."

I chiseled away a chunk of potato, about six inches long, only for something to catch my eye underneath.

There, carved into the cafeteria table, was the stick figure holding a spear.

"Ever seen this?" I asked.

"Looks like graffiti to me." Simms shrugged. "Why don't you clean that mashed crap up from the hallway?"

"It got in the hallway?"

"Boy—it got *everywhere*."

• • •

Wandering around school after dark was about as end-of-the-world as it gets. I could hear my steps echoing as I walked from one end of the hall to the other.

It felt like being the last person on the planet.

I called out—"Hey!"

Only to hear my voice bounce back at me:

Hey!

Hey.

Hey . . .

Assistant Principal Pritchard had informed me that I wouldn't be going home until the entire building was utterly spud-free. I had already called Mom to tell her I'd be late.

"Hey, Mom," I had said. "I'm thinking about sticking around after school today. Catch up on some studying."

"Let me guess: you're in detention?"

"Yep—you got it."

"What did you do this time?"

"Can I tell you when I get home?"

"Can't wait," she sighed. "Call when you need me to pick you up."

It was seven o'clock now. Mr. Simms and I had been the only people in the building for a while.

It was a pretty safe bet there'd be no potato-based smears in the library, but Mr. Simms told me to check, so here I was.

". . . Hello? Anybody in here?"

The hum of the florescent lights filled the room, and I ambled down a corridor of books, running my finger across a row of hardbacks.

What have we got here?

Fiddlers of the Civil War.

Stimulating.

I pulled it off the shelf, and discovered a pair of eyes blinking back at me from the neighboring aisle.

"Aaaah!"

I am not proud to admit that I screamed, lost my balance, and stumbled onto the bookcase behind me. I tried grabbing hold of any book that would keep me from falling but took a whole shelf to the floor instead.

Somebody was here.

In the next aisle.

"Kill the pig. . . ."

The voice barely rose above a raspy whisper, like gravel at the back of somebody's throat.

"Cut his throat. . . ."

I turned the corner, quick—but nobody was there. I spun back, half expecting to find my mysterious library companion creeping up behind me.

"Who is that? Who's there?"

"Spill his bloooood. . . ."

I stood. Waiting. Counting the seconds in my head:

Five, six, seven, eight—

Something whisked past my face and struck the spine of a copy of *European Fur-Trading: 1811.* My eyes refocused on a long slender spear jabbed into the book right in front of my nose.

Wait. This was no ordinary spear.

This was a *ruler.* A yardstick, actually.

Somebody had made a harpoon by strapping a run-of-the-mill, right-out-of-geometry-class drafting compass to the tip.

"We're coming for you," the voice whispered. *"And we're getting closer. . . ."*

Before I could blink, another spear whizzed past—nicking the lower lobe of my ear before impaling a copy of *Muskrats of South America.*

Yeeeeeow—that *hurt!*

I cupped my palm over the lobe to make sure it was still attached to my head. It felt wet. Bringing my hand up to my face, I could see I was bleeding.

This is not how I want to get my ears pierced.

As soon as I saw blood, dizziness took full effect. The room started to spin.

I was under attack. I had no idea who was doing it.

But I wasn't going to stick around and find out.

I booked it.

Ha—get it? *Booked it?* Even in trying times, it's good to have a sense of humor.

I ran so fast, I almost missed the silhouette racing alongside me in the next aisle.

Turning to my right, I saw another silhouette.

There were *two* of them.

That's when it dawned on me. These two were going to try to cut me off. I had to get to the exit before they did.

I pumped my legs harder, and the burning started in my chest.

Asthma. It felt like I'd been kicked in the lungs by a bucking bronchospasm.

Hey, airways, now's really not the time for an attack. Work with me here!

Forget about breathing. If I didn't get out of the library, I wasn't going to inhale oxygen ever again.

I felt a sharp sting at the back of my neck. I swatted to find a paper clip—*a paper clip?*—sticking out of my skin.

There was a sputtering behind me, followed by another sting on my shoulder.

Darts made from unfolded paper clips?

Whoever these library predators were, they were turning regular school supplies into artillery.

"Kill the pig!" one of them yelled. *"Cut his throat! Spill his blood!"*

They were close. I could almost feel their breath against my neck.

Only three steps away from the exit. My throat tightened, cutting off the air to my lungs.

One step . . .

Two steps . . .

Three . . .

I was about to clear the aisle, one leap between me and freedom, only . . .

Something snagged my foot.

I went down, *hard*, face-first to the floor.

Panicked, I flipped over. A jump rope was strung between separate bookshelves.

A trip wire.

Just as quickly as I saw it, the rope slackened and disappeared between books. *Gone.*

Trapped, I pinched my eyes shut and a hand grabbed my shoulder.

I screamed.

Again.

"What's wrong?" I opened my eyes to discover Mr. Simms leaning over me.

"They're after me! They're after me!"

"Who?"

"*Them.* They're right behind me. . . ."

Mr. Simms looked as startled as I felt. He peered down the aisle. "I don't see anybody."

I got up, refusing to believe him.

"Your ear's bleeding."

The library was completely empty. Silent except for the hum of florescent lights.

"They were here just a second ago. . . ."

"Ain't nobody here, son."

ASSEMBLY (OF THE DEAD)

Another bit of advice for all you newbies: *Always have an exit strategy.*

A few weeks had passed since the library attack. My injuries had finally healed, the last of my detentions served.

While in my after-school imprisonment, bored out of my brain, I had found a copiously underlined copy of *The Adventures of Tom Sawyer* behind my chair.

I would've sworn it hadn't been there before. It was almost like it had dropped out from the sky.

Or the ceiling, perhaps?

I flipped through it for a while, reading an underlined passage: "Best of all, the departed were the talk of the whole town. . . ."

But you know what? I found myself drifting away from the pages.

I'm *pro*-book, not a book*worm*.

There's a difference.

Now, finally as a free man, whenever I entered a room, my first order of business was always to quickly determine the best way to get the heck out.

Leap out the window? *Check.*

Climb through ventilation ducts in the ceiling? *Check.*

Dig a hole through the linoleum and tunnel into the sewer system toward safety? If worse comes to absolute worst . . . *Check.*

But wouldn't you know it?

Nothing happened.

No sneak attacks. No shifting fiberglass panels. No peeking eyes. No disappearing feet.

Nothing.

Save for the occasional shuffling sounds from the ceiling, we were in the midst of complete radio silence.

All's quiet on the educational front.

To be honest, things had gotten kind of boring. School had become, well, school again.

Thank the heavens for Halloween.

•••

Sarah Haversand came dressed as a unicorn. She'd taped a paper-towel tube wrapped in tinfoil to her forehead. At first glance, she looked like a horse impaled by a metal pole.

"You sure you're not a pony with a toilet-paper holder growing out of your skull?" I asked.

"I'm a unicorn, butt-mulch." She rolled her eyes. "Get away from me."

Halloween landed on a Thursday, which meant kids could wear costumes to school and parade through the halls in whatever getup they could pull together.

Lotta vampires. Lotta witches.

Not nearly enough zombies.

So I took it upon myself to imagine everybody dressed up as undead whatevers. Instead of Sarah Haversand being a unicorn, she was a *zombie* unicorn.

There were zombie princesses. Zombie cheerleaders.

Zombie ninjas, zombie prom queens, zombie zombies.

Everybody went from beyond boring to being a shuffling horde of flesh-eating preteens.

Now I know what you're asking yourself: *What awesome costume did you come up with?*

I'll give you one hint: It starts with a *Z* and ends with an *E*.

• • •

I'd slaved over the stove the night (of the Living Dead) before, boiling up a batch of linguine. I'd skinned every last tomato Mom had bought for the pasta sauce we would no longer be eating for dinner that evening, on account of the fact that I was using them for my guts.

"Um . . . Spencer?" Mom had asked. "What are you doing?"

"Getting my costume ready for tomorrow."

"Do I really want to know what an entire box of spaghetti has to do with your costume?"

"Probably not."

"Fair enough," she said. "I'll leave you to it, then."

I left the pasta in the fridge to cool, woke up at the crack of dawn (of the Dead), and dumped the tomatoes and pasta into a Ziploc bag. Then I took a whole roll of duct tape and strapped the bag underneath my shirt. That way, at school, I could rip open the Ziploc whenever I wanted and yank out my bloodsoaked entrails with my bare hands.

A couple dabs of baby powder to bleach out my skin, a few strokes of Mom's blush under my eyes—and voila: *Instant zombie.*

Go on. You can say it: Best. Zombie. *Ever.*

• • •

When third period rolled around, Assistant Principal Pritchard made the announcement for everybody to make their way to the gymnasium.

Finally. The moment we'd all been waiting for: costume competition time.

Every contestant would stand before the school and show off their getup.

I was a shoo-in for first prize. Total no-brainer.

Riley Callahan had dressed up as—surprise: a zombie Riley Callahan. The pink scar from his busted bottom lip gave him a permanent pouting expression, no matter what he was doing with his not-so-perfect-anymore face.

As we passed each other, I could tell Riley was too nervous to get anywhere near me. He had brought along a couple extra henchmen for protection, surrounding himself with so many Cro-Magnon photocopies that you would've thought a preppie parade of kids dressed in Riley costumes was marching through the hallway.

Riley took one look at me and asked, "Did you raid your dad's closet for that costume?"

"Don't talk about my dad."

"Why? Is he dead or something? Sure looks like it. . . ."

Keep it together, Spence.

I'd only get one shot at tearing open my stomach and spilling my entrails all over Riley—and you better believe I wanted to do it in front of as many people as possible.

That meant I had to:

1. Wait for the costume contest.
2. Find Riley in the front row.
3. Then he's all yours, Spencer.

Before I realized what he was up to, Riley grabbed hold of My Little Friend. He gave it a good yank, snapping the string around my neck.

"Let's see how long you can hold your breath without this. . . ."

"Give it back!"

Riley lobbed My Little Friend over my head to Riley Copy #1. By the time I caught up to R.C. #1, he had already tossed it to R.C. #2, who then flung it to R.C. #3.

Next thing you know, there's a game of monkey-in-the-middle going on in the hallway with yours truly fumbling through the flow of students, trying to catch my inhaler.

"I said—*give it back!*"

"Be careful not to panic, Spazzma." Riley laughed. "Don't want to give yourself an attack!"

I stopped floundering and stood before Riley. "Okay—*I'm sorry.* I apologize for everything I've ever done to you. Now, can I please have my inhaler back?"

"Tell you what"—Riley grinned—"I'll hold on to it until the end of the day. You can pick it up in the bus loop after school."

Riley and his boys pushed their way into the gymnasium, laughing, as I stood there letting everybody pass and trying hard to balance my breathing.

Werekids in crappy costumes kept filing around me.

Zombie wizards. Zombie pirates.

Zombie tribesman.

Tribesman?

Somebody bumped my shoulder. I turned to see who it was, figuring one of Riley's Cro-Magnon copies was back for another rousing round of ragging-on-Spencer.

But it wasn't a member of his crew.

It was a chubby kid I'd never seen before.

He was wearing the Greenfield gym uniform. Only, the letters had faded and his shirt had been ripped, then put back together with a staggering amount of safety pins. It was as if he'd been wearing it for years and never once taken it off.

Not the most inventive costume. But I gave him points for the concept.

There were a half dozen gym whistles wrapped around his neck. And a row of plastic sporks lined the length of his chest like a bandolier.

He seemed a little . . . off.

The glint in his eyes was totally giving me wild-child vibes. He looked older than most students, like he'd been held back a few too many times. There was something written on his fingers—letters tattooed on each knuckle. His left fist said . . .

S

P

O

R

Staring me down, the boy balled both hands, bringing them together.

SPORKBOY

"Trick or treat," he taunted. "Smell my feet, give me something good to eat. . . ."

The last of the costumed students trickled by, and I turned, intending to make a break for it, only to run face-first into a wall in the middle of the hallway.

But it wasn't a wall.

It was a person.

A very *tall* person.

I craned my neck up to a tower of a kid looking down at me. A sharpened yardstick hung off of each hip. He made eye contact briefly, then looked away and presented his knuckles to me. I could barely make out the word scrawled across his skin:

YARDSTICK

Whoever he was, he'd dreaded his hair. Not "dread" as in "be afraid of it," but as in he had knotted his hair into these thick tendrils on top of his head. He'd adorned each lock with items from around school: lost earrings, safety pins, even a key that had probably been plucked from Mr. Simms's retractable keychain.

By now, all the other students were in the gym, so it was just me—and them.

A third tribesman stepped up, seemingly out of nowhere. Same ratty, pinned-together gym clothes. His face was a supernova of acne, and in his hands rested a pair of plastic protractors, each semicircular edge sporting a line of X-ACTO blades. His bandolier held a gleaming row of compasses.

Glaring wildly, he smashed his fists together. His knuckles read:

COMPASS

"Who . . . ?" I started, but couldn't finish.

Silence.

"Who . . . ?" I tried again, my chest beginning to burn.

Bad time for an asthma attack.

I took a step back and bumped into somebody. I spun around. Another one?

He looked older than the rest. His nasal septum was pierced with a paper clip, the thin bit of metal running directly through the cartilage that divided his nostrils. His alabaster body left him looking like he hadn't seen sunlight in years. A belt of hollowed-out pens was wrapped around his waist.

Looking at his hands, I noticed they were letter-free. But a necklace of handwriting ringed his throat:

PEASHOOTER

"Who . . . ?" I tried one last time.

"Who . . ." he asked, "are we?" A smirk curled his lip. "We're your friends."

That's when I blacked out.

THE GIRL IN THE BOILER ROOM

Where was I? What happened?

First order of business: Get my head to stop spinning.

Second: Figure out why long strands of entrails are spilling out from this Grand Canyon–size rift in my stomach. And what are the squiggly bits that smell like the Olive Garden?

And how come I'm not dead yet?

Looking up, I saw a series of pipes and pressure valves hanging over my head. An odd metal contraption next to me hissed, spitting slips of steam into the air.

The boiler room? It had to be.

Someone was kneeling next to me.

A girl.

She was about my age, maybe a little older, but it was hard to tell. Her hair covered most of her face. She was wearing a mismatch of old clothes held together by an exoskeleton of safety pins.

And she was staring at my stomach, sniffing.

Literally.

She dipped her pinkie into my guts, wriggled it around, and brought it up to her mouth, lightly tapping it to her tongue.

"You're . . . Italian?"

Cannibals.

There were cannibals running around our school.

And I was their next meal.

My esophagus cinched shut.

This was not how I had planned to spend third period. Mr. Rorshuck was going to think I was skipping his class—when, in reality, I was asphyxiating directly below his feet in the basement of the building.

I grabbed at my neck, but My Little Friend wasn't there.

Riley.

"Do you need an inhaler?" Cannibal Girl asked. All I could do was nod—*Yes! Yes! Yes!*

She turned and rushed toward a pile of inhalers stacked in a far corner.

Wait. Why was there a stockpile of asthma medicine stashed in the basement of Greenfield Middle School?

Cannibal Girl ran back and held out an inhaler. I grabbed it, brought it up to my mouth, and squeezed.

Empty.

Cannibal Girl rushed back to the pile of inhalers and grabbed another one. She shook it, then tossed it over her shoulder and reached for another.

Please, oh please, tell me they're not all empty.

"Found one!"

I couldn't even grab the inhaler. She had to bring it up to my mouth, prying apart my lips and pushing the button down.

Air. Sweet medicated air . . .

"Are you okay?" Cannibal Girl hovered above me and swept the hair out of her face. Her pale skin was like marble. White marble with the faintest trace of blue veins.

She suddenly looked familiar to me.

Where have I seen her before?

"Why do you have a bag of spaghetti taped to your stomach?" she asked.

Whoops.

So those *weren't* my guts hanging everywhere. Maybe this girl wasn't a cannibal after all.

"I brought these for you." She nodded to the stockpile of inhalers.

It was then that I noticed all the other piles stowed around the room. Stashes of school supplies, each type categorized and stacked in its own mountain. I was up to my knees in the world's most meticulous lost-and-found collection.

Textbooks

Old library books

Whistles

Cafeteria trays

Money

Plastic cutlery

And my personal weapon of choice—staplers. Lots of staplers.

You name it. All here in nice little heaps.

"Who are you?" I finally mustered.

"Sully."

In an instant, a million little black dots formed into a perfect constellation of her face.

"Sully Tulliver?"

"You . . . you know who I am?"

I was about to nod yes, when guess who got whacked on the back of his head?

Just when I'd found her, somebody had to sneak up from behind and bludgeon me with what felt like the world's biggest math textbook. Knocked out cold.

That's one way to cram for class.

PIÑATA
DE
CARNE

 could feel the blood rushing to my head before I opened my eyes.

Sure enough, I came to—hanging upside down.

I'd been strung up to a basketball hoop in our gymnasium. There was a jump rope wrapped around the lower half of my legs and tied to the rim. Another jump rope, looped around my torso, held my arms in place.

I felt like a carcass hanging from a butcher's meat hook.

A meat piñata.

Not a pretty picture, I know.

I spotted the clock on the gym wall. It was only—10:30 a.m.? *Wait.* Hold up. That would mean it was still third period. Where was the Halloween assembly?

But I was upside down. It was really 6:50 p.m. School had been over for nearly four hours! The only sign that the costume competition had come and gone were candy corns littering the gym floor, looking like the lost fangs of a few dozen werekids. Just one more mess for Mr. Simms to pick up.

I tried to yell for help, but there was something stuffed inside my mouth.

All I could do was wriggle my hands at my waist. I started to panic. None of this hypothetical maybe-this-is-all-just-a-dream kind of panic, but the oh-I-think-I-just-pooped-in-my-pants kind.

Remain calm, Spencer, I said to myself. *Think.* How are you going to get out of this one?

I heard a door open behind me, which sent an echo through the empty gym. I tried to turn my head around to see who was coming, but I was dangling in the wrong direction.

I saw bare feet first.

They were hovering just above—*below*—me, five sets, each attached to people wearing safety-pinned gym uniforms. Even though their feet were planted firmly on the floor, they looked like a row of wax-skinned bats hanging from the three-point line.

I had to tilt my head to the side just to get a good look at them—and when I did, I realized there was writing all over their bodies. I got lost reading the scribbled bits of graffiti wrapped around their arms and legs.

LOST BOY

WHITE FANG

ADVERTISE HERE

The one with the paper clip nose-piercing stepped forward.

"*I blacken the name of our fair city . . .*" he recited. "*I beat up people. . . . I am a menace to society. Man, do I have fun!*"

Say—*what?*

"Call me Peashooter."

The tall one with the yardsticks stepped up next. He had measured and marked a column of perpendicular lines across the length of his legs to correspond with the metric system—inches, centimeters, and millimeters. His legs looked like a pair of rulers.

He murmured something I couldn't quite make out.

"You're lard sick?" I managed to ask through my gag.

"Yardstick." He raised his voice. "I'm *Yardstick.*"

The one with the acne had sketched the symbol of an atom across one forearm, while the image of a drafting compass piercing an anatomically correct heart was drawn on the other.

"Call me Compass."

The next to step forward had *LORD OF THE FRIES* scrawled across the slope of his belly in a meticulously executed Old English font. There was a skull and crossbones on his forearm. *Wait*—scratch that. Not crossbones. A fork and knife.

"The name's Sporkboy," he declared as he drum-rolled his own stomach. "Got a problem with that?"

Again with the crazy eyes.

I shook my head—*nope.*

"Good."

Each was wearing about six different whistles, like strings of silver teeth dangling across their chests.

And they'd armed themselves.

Compasses bent open to expose their sharp points.

X-ACTO blades attached to protractors.

Sharpened pencils.

I saw Sully standing at the back. She was one of the posse. The only girl among the boys. Her choice in clothes differed from theirs. And no writing anywhere I could see. Her head hung low enough for her hair to cover most of her face, but I saw her eyes peering through.

"What are you looking at?" she asked. "You already know my name."

I stared back at her with pleading eyes: *Help help help help help*—but she didn't seem to receive my message.

Or want to.

I could almost trace the veins running the length of her pale limbs, and her eyes were overly dilated.

Like cat eyes.

Peashooter leaned over until we were face-to-face. I noticed something in his hand.

Something small.

With teeth.

He held out his hand so that I could get a good look-see.

A staple remover—a four-fanged pincer with spring-locked

jaws—was an inch away from my nose. Without saying anything, he slipped its metallic teeth into my nostrils, and pinched.

Not enough to break the skin. No nosebleeds here. But enough to get my attention.

I was all ears.

"Everybody's gone for the day." He tugged harder. "Nobody'll hear you."

He released my nose so that I rocked back and forth from the basketball rim. Then he caught me by the nose again, pinching me in place.

"If I remove your gag, you better not scream. Promise?"

I nodded. *Slowly.*

He detached his staple remover from my nose again. He sunk its fangs into the wad in my mouth and tugged it out.

A sock. I'd had a dirty gym sock stuffed in my mouth this whole time.

I took a deep breath, then emptied all that fresh air from my lungs by yelling my head off: "Help me help me help me somebody please get me out of here help help help!"

Nothing. No cavalry to save the day.

"Told you nobody would hear," Peashooter said. "Now you've gotta pay for your disloyalty. . . ."

Yardstick and Sporkboy each pulled out a sock stuffed with something that appeared to be heavy. Sporkboy started swinging his over his head like a helicopter propeller, sending a slight clink-clinking sound through the air.

They must've been filled with spare change.

By my hasty calculations, about fifty-seven cents of pain each. *Give or take.*

"Pound him," Peashooter nodded.

In the blink of an eye, both boys advanced and proceeded to whack me as hard as they could. The thud of money against my body brought the holler right out of me: "Ow ow ow!"

"Never break your promises. Not to us, got it? *Word is bond.*"

I gasped. "What do you want from me?"

"We tied you up to see how you'd handle yourself."

"This is some kind of *test*? Did I pass?"

"Hardly," Compass huffed, the acne spread across his face reddening.

"I'm getting really light-headed up here. . . ."

Sully rushed up and brought an inhaler to my mouth. She squeezed off a gust into my lungs.

"Somebody's got a crush." Sporkboy snorted. Compass laughed along with him.

Out of nowhere, Sully brandished a slingshot. Before Sporkboy could even blink, she'd loaded a penny, aimed, and fired.

Bull's-eye—right in the navel.

"Owww! I was just joking."

"For the female of the species is more deadly than the male," Sully recited.

"Who the heck said that?" Sporkboy rubbed his sore tummy.

"Rudyard Kipling."

"Yeah, well—*For a penny in the belly isn't as painful as my fist in your face,*" he spat back. "That was *me*. I said that!"

"Enough!" Peashooter silenced the two of them. He then turned back to me. "We've had our eyes on you for some time."

"What did I do?"

"We know you're looking for an escape."

Escape?

With all the blood in my body rushing to my skull, I was having a full-blown hallucination. Either that, or this had just become the weirdest Halloween of my life.

"The time to rise is nearly upon us." Peashooter gnashed the teeth of his staple remover in front of my face. "Who will you stand by? Us—or the cattle you call classmates? You have been chosen to join our tribe. *To become one of us!*"

Along his left forearm, I could read *DAMAGE DONE*.

This can't be happening.

Sporkboy lunged forward, and I flinched, thinking he was about to bludgeon me with his sock cudgel again, but Peashooter held out his hand, halting him.

"Enough."

"Come on," Sporkboy whined. "Let me just have a little fun with him. . . ."

Peashooter leaned into my face.

"We can do anything we want here." He grinned. "This is our home."

Sully leaned over, whispering, "It can be your home too."

"Think about it," Peashooter said. "We'll be back for you."

"When?"

"Soon."

Peashooter stuffed the sock into my mouth before it even dawned on me to ask him to cut me down.

• • •

Mr. Simms wheeled his mop and bucket into the gym. I could hear his key chain rattling at his hip ahead of seeing him.

"What the—?" he started.

"*Mmm-mff mmff-mmm!*"

Rough translation: *Get me down from here before my head pops like a tick fattened up on too much blood!*

"What's going on here?" he asked, tugging the sock from my mouth.

"Keep it down!" I gasped. "They're watching. . . ."

"What are you talking about?" Mr. Simms pulled out his pocketknife and started sawing through the jump rope around my torso. "Who did this?"

"Headhunters!"

"Head—*what?*"

Done with the first rope, he started on the one suspended from the basketball rim and soon sent me splatting against the gymnasium floor.

Ouch! My body felt like a slab of beef after a few hours with a meat tenderizer.

"You've got to believe me," I said, slowly regaining my equilibrium. "Somewhere in this school there's a tribe of teenage headhunters!"

Mr. Simms gave me a look I was a little too familiar with. He wasn't buying a word of what I'd said.

"Headhunters? In . . . school?"

"Yes! Well. Sort of."

Mr. Simms didn't say anything for a long time.

"You don't believe me?" I said.

"Would you?"

He had a point.

• • •

Mom hugged me so tight, I think she may have broken a couple of my ribs. Tears ran down her cheeks. I don't think she'd ever been this happy to see me before.

Then she gripped my shoulders and shook me until whiplash was inevitable. Fury flashed through her face, eclipsing her relief. "*Spencer Austin Pendleton!*"

You know you're in big trouble when your mother pulls out your middle name.

"I called the police. I had no idea what had happened to you—"

"I'm sorry, Mom—"

"Don't you ever, *ever* do something like this to me again!"

"I said I was sorry!"

Mr. Simms stepped up, coughing lightly. "You know how boys get, ma'am. Kids'll start fooling around, and before you know it, there goes the time."

Mom let me go, turning her attention toward him.

"Thank you for keeping an eye on him, Mr. . . ."

"Simms." He held out his hand and shook Mom's. "Wasn't any hassle, really. You got a good kid here, no matter how much of a headache he can be."

"I'd say he's a full-on migraine most days."

"Mom . . ."

"This was the last place I figured I'd find you. What were you doing at school?"

Mr. Simms and I exchanged a quick glance as I considered telling her the truth. That I had been kidnapped by a tribe of wild kids living in the school who wanted to recruit me?

Who was I kidding?

"Oh, you know," I said. "Just hanging out with some new friends."

Part II: November

Be careful what you wish for, 'cause you just might get it. . . .
—Eminem

PEP RALLY (OF THE UNDEAD)

Schools look exactly the same no matter where you go. Greenfield Middle was no different.

Same endless hallways that reach from one end of the building to the other.

Same flickering florescent lights buzzing like bug zappers, sucking the energy from my skull: *Bzzst-bzzst!*

We may as well have been moths fluttering toward electrified deaths: *Bzzzzzzzzzzst!*

The only thing that had changed was my locker, which was never where it was supposed to be. Or where I thought it was supposed to be.

Next to the gymnasium? *Nope.*

The cafeteria? *Nope.*

Library? *Sorry—try again.*

Another thing that remained the same as my last school was

my leprous rep. Contrary to popular belief, being a boat-rock-star only racked up temporary celebrity points.

What's the old saying?

The more things change, the more nobody knows my name?

For a while, whenever I passed a pack of werekids, their eyes would tighten at the sight of me, as if my mere presence was an insult to their lycanthropic clique.

A few weeks into November and none of them even looked at me anymore.

I was a ghost.

Fine by me.

I'd survive.

Somebody had drawn a doodle of my face on the front of my locker, with a spear running through my ears and my brain dangling off the bloodied tip by its cerebral cortex.

Below it, in bold block letters, it read: *EYES ON YOU.*

It was written in permanent marker, so I doubted it'd be coming off anytime soon.

Sorry, Mr. Simms. . . .

Once I got the books I needed, I slammed the metal door shut and came face-to-face with a grizzly bear.

You heard right: *a grizzly bear.*

The overinflated head of our school mascot, Griz the Grizzly, popped out of nowhere, like he'd been hiding behind my locker door, ready to pounce.

"Don't do that!"

Griz's plastic eyes stared blankly back at me—or, more precisely, *over* me.

"You take this job way too seriously, Martin. . . ."

Martin Mendleson always volunteered to slip into Greenfield's mascot costume during pep rallies.

"Pep rally's in the gym," I said. "Better head over before Pritchard wonders where you've wandered off to."

Heavy breathing seeped through the wire mesh of Griz's mouth.

"You okay, Martin? You sound sick. . . ."

There was definitely something different about Martin. Usually he was a little more animated when he wore this getup.

"Martin?"

Nothing.

"Ha-ha, Martin."

Then from inside Griz's mouth, I heard, *"Kill the pig."*

Even though it was barely above a whisper, I could make out the slightest giggle. Whoever was settled inside this bear's belly, it definitely wasn't Martin.

Griz stood there staring until I made out the eyes inside the mask's mouth.

Sporkboy.

"Meet us under the bleachers."

That's when Riley Callahan and his crew waltzed up and slapped the mascot upside his fuzzy head. "What're you two lovebirds up to? Making plans for the winter formal?"

Griz just stared blankly.

"Hey, Riley," the voice inside said. "What's that smell?"

Before Riley could reply, a fart erupted from deep within the bear's plush bowels. Noxious fumes seeped through the wire mesh mouth, straight into Riley's face.

Perfect opportunity for me to make my exit.

With Riley and his crew gagging on poisonous grizzly-bear vapors, I slipped off into the gymnasium.

Thanks for cutting the mustard gas, Griz. . . .

• • •

Fact: Middle-school pep rallies are never enjoyable.

What's fun about being forced to sit through a lame attempt at getting the student body riled up about something as abysmal as middle-school sports?

First, the Greenfield cheerleading squad would stumble through some half-rehearsed routine, chanting, "BE AGGRESSIVE! B-E AGGRESSIVE!"

Then the band would blast through some *rah-rah-sis-boom-belch*.

And then you have to suffer through some prepackaged spiel by the assistant principal about leading your basketball/football/baseball/numbskull team to victory.

You love pep rallies?

To each his own.

Below the bleachers, the sound of pounding feet was deafening, like a thousand students were marching on my head. I had slipped into the latticework of scaffolding that held up the risers, and had a perfect view of hundreds upon hundreds of shoes, all stomping simultaneously.

A cattle stampede of herd mentality.

Spurred on by the chant of cheerleaders: "B-E A-G-G-R-E-S-S-I-V-E!"

Sounds like they're out for blood.

And there they were—perched on the metal framework that held up the bleachers. From their own personal ringside seats, they stared through the gaps in the risers.

Peashooter gave a quick nod. His paper-clip piercing had a shine to it, even in the shadows. I could just make out the tattoos on his arm. They had changed. Now cursive letters wrapped the length of his right arm like ivy: *THE ARTFUL DODGER.*

Pretty cool.

I found a spot on a metal bar covered in scabs of bubble gum, next to Sully. Her hair was hiding most of her face, but I could see her eyes peering out.

"Funny bumping into you down here," I said. "How did you score such good seats?"

"What did you just call me?" she asked, her voice competing with the pounding of feet. I saw her hand graze her slingshot.

"No." I leaned into her ear. "I said: It's good. To see. You."

Compass hissed at me, acne flaring up, and pressed his index finger against his lips. His right arm now read *GUINEA PIG* in bold block letters. Once I was sufficiently shushed, he took his finger and pointed toward the basketball court.

I turned to look.

Our assistant principal had stepped up to the microphone at the center line, flanked by a V-formation of pom-pom girls. He cued the band behind him to stop, with a wave of his hand.

"Thank you," he said as the instruments faded. "I have a few general announcements before the fun begins. As a lot of you know, our winter concert is coming up and. . . ."

But no one was watching Pritchard.

All eyes were focused on Griz waddling up behind him. The bear began to moonwalk across the court, causing some in the crowd to giggle.

"This year's concert will be held right here in the—"

Confused, Pritchard stopped and turned around to see what was so funny. The band thought this was their cue to start playing again, and launched into the next song.

Peashooter nodded at Compass as the music got louder. Compass nodded back.

What are they up to?

I suddenly spotted the umpteen thin-wicked, round red pellets taped to nearly every bracket of scaffolding. How I hadn't noticed them before was beyond me.

B-E P-E-R-C-E-P-T-I-V-E, Spence.

Peashooter pointed to a door tucked behind the bleachers with the word BASEMENT stenciled across the front.

Am I supposed to book it to the boiler room?

Before I could ask, Peashooter had lit the first smoke bomb with a match.

Compass lit the wicks lining his section.

So did Yardstick.

Sully pulled out her slingshot and slipped a lit smoke bomb into a little leather pouch. As she aimed, I took a better look at her weapon of choice. The forked frame was a pair of safety scissors, open and locked into place with the blades duct-taped together to form a handle. She had tied off a braided belt of rubber bands through the scissor's finger rings.

One eye closed, Sully took aim—and fired.

Her smoke bomb shot out from beneath the bleachers, a trail of red streaking across the basketball court, and landed in the bell of a tuba. The poor kid playing it burped out one last gaseous note before crimson fumes spewed from the rotund funnel, like a tomato fart.

You definitely don't see something like that every day.

Scattered coughing spread over our heads. You could hear the confusion as werekids began to question one another: "What's going on? What's happening? Is the gym on fire?"

At the mention of *fire*, the word began to sweep from mouth to mouth—until it lit everybody's tongue. "Fire? Fire!? FIRE!"

"Remain calm," Pritchard stammered into the mic. "Everybody walk single file to your closest exit in a calm, collected manner. . . ."

But it was too late.

The sound of pounding feet picked up again, only this time, there was no rhythm. The tempo was pure panic as werekids raced for the exits.

No one in the frightened stampede could hear the Tribe beneath their thundering feet, chanting along with the chaos—"BE AGGRESSIVE! B-E AGGRESSIVE!"

"B-E A-G-G-R-E-S-S-I-V-E!"

LAY OF THE LAND

Smoke rises," Sully yelled over the commotion. "Keep your head down and follow me."

While the rest of the student body blindly collided into one another escaping a blanket of colored smoke, I scuttled to the basement with the Tribe.

"We heard you burned your last school to the ground." Sporkboy had Griz's head tucked under his arm, and he was plucking tufts of fur off its face. "Sounds like a flat-out fib to me. . . ."

"What? You think I made it up?"

"What about stapling Pritchard's hand to his desk?" Compass asked. "Are you gonna cop to that too—or is it just another tall tale?"

"Yeah, I took Pritchard down."

Sully snorted. "Looked more like you lost your balance to me."

"Wait . . . that was *you* in the ceiling?"

"Surprise."

"We are the eyes and ears of this place," Peashooter said. "If anything happens, we're there."

"Why?" I asked. "I mean . . . what are you guys doing here?"

Fair question, right?

"Take a look." Peashooter craned his neck. "What do you see?"

"School?"

"We see a fortress. A castle. A sanctuary."

"So the school's your own personal clubhouse?" I asked. "And here I thought it was just another boring building."

"To everybody else it is." Peashooter lifted his chin. "But for us, *it's home.*"

"What about TV?"

"No television." Compass shook his head. "No cell phones. No video games."

"And cafeteria grub for the rest of your lives?"

"You get used to it," Sporkboy said as he rubbed his tummy.

"Sloppy joes from now to the day you die?" I asked. "Really?"

"Nobody out there cared about us," Peashooter said. "There was nowhere in the outside world that we felt like we could call home. *But this is ours.*"

"And if you get caught?"

"Nobody knows we're here."

"*I* know."

"Because we let you."

"Why?" I asked. "Why choose me?"

Peashooter grinned as if he'd been waiting for me to ask him that all day long. I couldn't help but get a little nervous. He raised his arms over his head and took in a deep breath.

"You've fought forgotten ancestors," he recited. *"They've quickened the old life within you, the old tricks which they've stamped into the heredity of the breed are your tricks."*

"Uh . . ." I couldn't help but stare. "What's that supposed to mean?"

"You've got potential," Peashooter said. "We've seen it."

"You mean it's not my stunning good looks?"

Awkward silence.

The acne scattered across Compass's face deepened in color like some kind of poisonous deep-sea coral. He spoke first, not amused. "It's your skill with manipulating information."

"Sounds like you're calling me a liar."

"Not a liar." Peashooter shook his head. *"A public relations specialist."*

"You want me to be your tribal press agent?"

"More like minister of information," Compass suggested.

"You've got to be kidding. . . ."

"No modern war has been won without managing the distribution of information," Peashooter said. "Besides, somebody's got to record what happens here for those who come after us. Like Winston Churchill said, 'History is written by the victors.'"

War? Victors? He can't be serious.

Peashooter continued. "Our war is against the status quo. The state of affairs as the students in this school know it. We know you want to shake things up just as much as we do. Just one look at your clashes in class and it's easy to see whose side you're on."

"Which side is that?"

"We saw you handle Mrs. Witherspoon," he said. "You whipped up that bogus oral report on the Swanahanzi headhunters on the fly, didn't you? Just think what you could do for us."

"You guys don't need a minister of fibs," I said. "What you need is a tailor. You look like some postapocalyptic, dystopian athletic squad. . . ."

"You really think that matters to us?" Compass asked. The slightest whiff of superiority escaped in his tone. "We don't have to fit in anymore."

"Don't you want to—I don't know—*grow up*? Go to high school? Get a driver's license?"

"And then what?" Peashooter asked. "Graduate? Get a job you hate? Get married and have a family you only see on weekends until you get divorced and retire and end up looking back at your boring, worthless life and realize that it was never your life to begin with?"

"Who says that's the way it's got to be?"

"Isn't it for your parents?" Peashooter shot back, his paperclip piercing twitching.

Quick. Change the subject.

"What about you?" I nodded to Yardstick. He'd been quiet this whole time, reflexively rolling the corkscrews of his hair. "Ever get homesick?"

"This is home," he whispered.

"Don't you miss your families?"

"This is our family," Sully said.

"Odd family."

"Maybe." Peashooter shrugged. "But we're happy. Can you say the same?"

Can I?

"Wanna play their game?" Peashooter asked. "Go ahead. Riley Callahan will always treat you like crap. Sarah Haversand will never know you exist. No one here will ever believe you. And then you have us—offering you the chance to actually be a part of something."

I pictured it in my head.

Me. Answering the call. Joining up. *Belonging* to something.

It would be like being thirteen forever.

And you want to know the crazy part?

What Peashooter was proposing didn't sound crazy at all.

Greenfield Middle School. Home, sweet home.

Kind of had a ring to it.

PEP RALLY (OF THE LIVING)

Better get back before anyone realizes you're missing," Peashooter said before he and the rest slipped into the shadows of the boiler room.

"I can't just go back to class," I protested. "It's already fourth period. Pritchard's probably pinning this all on me as we speak."

"You're a smart guy. Figure something out."

Before I could balk—he was gone. All of them were. It was as if they had disappeared into the walls of the building.

Now what was I supposed to do?

My brain sputtered out nothing but a series of brain farts. I was still in shock over their invitation into the seedy underbelly of disorganized academia.

Just tell the truth, a little voice at the back of my head peeped. *Absolve yourself.*

Yeah, but who's going to believe the truth when it's coming from you? I answered back. *I'm Public (Education) Enemy #1 now. Best to keep a low profile.*

I decided to head to the nurse's office and tell her I was feeling sick from smoke bomb inhalation. I was sure she'd write a pass to get me into my fifth period class.

Instant alibi.

Miss Braswell bought the act—hook, line, and *stinker.* I threw in a few coughs as well as a puff from My Little Friend for safe measure. She made me lie down on the vinyl bed for the rest of the period.

So far, my plan was working perfectly.

Just close your eyes until the bell rings. Take a nap.

Assistant Principal Pritchard's voice rumbled over the intercom. "I'd like to speak directly to the students responsible for today's incident in the gymnasium. . . ."

It was like the voice of God was speaking directly to me. And He didn't sound all that happy.

This isn't good.

"I'm offering you an opportunity to turn yourself in," Pritchard continued. "If you voluntarily come to my office before school ends, this will be seen as a willingness on your part to comply. If you don't, I cannot offer you any leniency when I find you. . . ."

Pritchard's voice thundered through school: "And rest assured, I will find you."

I'm in way over my head. What have I gotten myself into?

As if to validate my fears, the fiberglass panel over my head pulled back, and a folded piece of paper dropped onto the bed. The ceiling closed itself before Miss Braswell noticed.

I turned over onto my side and unfolded the note.

Two simple sentences: *Hide in the last stall in the boys' room. Wait there until we contact you.*

• • •

I had called home to tell Mom there was a basketball game at school that night. I'd get a ride home with some friends.

Friends. Mom should've seen right through that one.

My new "friends" had me huddled on a toilet seat, knees pressed against my chest, for what felt like hours.

Sitting in that silence, I was overcome by how quiet—how eerily soundless—the school could be when nobody was inside it.

Mausoleum quiet.

Necropolis quiet.

I peered between my feet, deep into the toilet bowl, where the white porcelain was swallowed by shadows.

I felt myself at the edge. One step forward and I'd be in a free fall forever.

It's not too late. You can still walk away from this.

Couldn't I?

Could I?

"Spencer?"

The voice from above my head startled me. Looking up, I discovered Sully.

"Everybody's gone," she said. "The place is ours."

• • •

Peashooter entered the center circle of the basketball court. Less than ten hours ago, Assistant Principal Pritchard had been run over on the very same spot by five hundred panicked students rushing for the door. Remnants of the stampede still remained: tossed-off pom-poms, crumpled notebook paper, an abandoned backpack.

Now Peashooter stood before the empty bleachers and grinned as if those empty rows of pine planks were the rib cage on a corpse pecked clean of its meat—and he was the vulture with the fullest tummy.

"When did you ever feel *school pride?*" His question ricocheted across the court. "When did this place ever make you feel like you belonged?"

There were only the five of us scattered about the gym—but from the boom of his voice, Peashooter may as well have been spurring on an army of hundreds.

"*Never.* That's when. And you know why . . . ? Because you *don't* belong."

Peashooter turned to Yardstick. Somehow, he had managed to scale one of the basketball backboards. Now he was using the basket as a seat, his scrawny butt crammed in the hoop, and his daddy longlegs dangling.

"You never belonged," Peashooter said directly to Yardstick. "Not to them. Not in this building. Not to anyone—but yourself."

Compass was sitting a few feet to my left. He was already riled up.

"There was a time when I walked among the student body of Greenfield wanting nothing more than to belong." Peashooter looked up toward the ceiling and shook his head. "I tried so hard. *And still*—I wasn't good enough. *And still*—they didn't care."

Sully sat to my right. I glanced over to see how she was reacting to all this, but there was no peeking through that eclipse of hair.

Peashooter continued. "But the joke was on me. On all of us—because we fell for it."

Sporkboy was in the front row, beaming like a teacher's pet with rabies. He picked up a discarded pom-pom, lit it on fire with a match, and tossed it high into the air.

Sully drew her slingshot and fired off a penny. *Direct hit!* The burning tassels burst into sparks, dissipating in the air like a dying Fourth of July firework.

"We tried their slave-brained way of life. But their lives aren't theirs at all! They've been conditioned, just like the students before them and the students before that. That's not school pride. That's what *lemmings* do."

Peashooter turned to Sporkboy.

"Remember what a lemming is?"

"It's a rat," Sporkboy promptly responded, pleased with himself for remembering his biology lesson. A wide grin spread across his face until his cheeks pinched his eyes.

"That's right." Peashooter nodded. "A stupid rodent that follows other stupid rodents. It's their nature to follow blindly, one after another, until they run off a cliff and drown in the sea. If the lemming ahead does it, so will the lemming behind. Every last one of them!"

Yardstick's legs began to swing through the air. Peashooter's speech was working its magic on him. On all of us. I imagined this was the Big Game and Peashooter was our coach, giving us our pep talk before hitting the field.

He was psyching us up for battle.

For war.

"This school? This school has no leaders. The sixth graders blindly follow the seventh graders, who blindly follow the eighth graders, who blindly march into high school. None of them, not one single student, stops to ponder what might happen if they were to break from the herd."

Peashooter paused and everything felt deathly quiet. All I could hear was the dull thud of my own heart pounding against my chest.

"Until now. *Until us.*"

Peashooter walked up to me. He continued to address everyone, but from the glint in his eye, I could tell this was meant particularly for my ears.

"No more GPA. No more aptitude testing or placement testing or cognitive testing or any of it. Because we are not grades!"

"*No!*" Sporkboy yelled back.

"We are not yearbook photos!"

"*No!*" Compass chimed in along with Sporkboy.

"We are not basketball starting lineups!"

"*No!*" Yardstick followed along with the others, their voices growing stronger. More confident.

"We are not status updates!"

"*No!*" Sully and I added to the chorus.

"We are free!" Peashooter raised his arms over his head. "Free to make a home for ourselves! Free to do what we want! To read what we want! To *belong* where we want! That's what true school spirit is. All that stands between us and making this school ours are the five hundred mindless rodents who follow each other from class to class, day in and day out. *Lemmings learning how to be better lemmings!*"

Sporkboy was the first to leap to his feet, charged. Yardstick hopped down from the backboard. Compass popped up from the bleachers and followed along.

Peashooter scanned their eager faces. He had them right where he wanted them.

I turned to Sully and discovered she was already standing.

I was the only one left.

"True school pride is emancipation from the herd. To shake up the status quo!"

Peashooter locked his eyes on mine. He held out his hand.

"I stand before you and declare that if you feel true school pride, then fight for it!"

I took Peashooter's hand. He pulled me up from the bleachers with such force, I felt like a basketball propelled across the court for a three-point shot.

Nothing but net.

"Fight for this school and make it ours!" Peashooter craned his neck back and shouted, "*To the law of claw and fang!*"

"*Claw and fang!*" we yelled in unison, our collective voice flooding the gym.

"*Claw and fang!*"

"*Claw and fang!*"

• • •

We took to the halls.

We ran from one end of the building to the other, whooping and leaping and colliding, and knocking over anything that got in our way.

We tore down banners proclaiming school pride.

We made our own proclaiming—SCHOOL LIED.

We raided the music room and paraded down the hallways celebrating our greatness as loudly as we could.

We loosened the screws on all the desks in Mr. Rorshuck's classroom and scribbled mathematical profanities across his blackboard: *Testiclation! Assiom! Isuckeles triangle!*

This is for calling us names.

We TP'ed the hallways. We mummified the main office. We shrouded the library.

We decimated the Dewey decimal system as Peashooter shouted, "Take reading back from the bookworms! Take our books back from these maggots!"

We raided the food storage and ate with our bare hands.

We took a garbage bin from the cafeteria and stuffed as much putrid food into Riley Callahan's broken-in locker as it could hold.

This is for taunting us.

We reset all the clocks. We adjusted them to totally random hours, tangling up the minutes until there was no synchronicity, no uniformity, as if to say, *Now it's our time.*

We unscrewed globes from their mounts and played dodgeball with the world.

We took the chalk—every last bit from the building—and flushed it down the toilet.

This is for everything.

This is for nothing.

We broke into the track-and-field supply closet and took whatever equipment we wanted.

We spiked javelins into the ground at the front entrance, then impaled a red rubber dodgeball on each.

Let these faceless decapitated heads serve as a warning: *Beware all ye who enter here.*

Sully began to chant, jumping up and down in mock-cheerleader fashion: "BE AGGRESSIVE!"

We lifted our javelins and our voices in chorus: "B-E AGGRESSIVE!"

I found myself chanting loudest: *"B-E A-G-G-R-E-S-S-I-V-E!"*

We were wild. We were free.

We were home.

• • •

It was one in the morning by the time I left school.

How had it gotten so late?

I had to hoof it home, which would give me just enough time to come up with a good excuse.

Get brainstorming, Spencer. You'll need a whopper for this one.

When the headlights hit me, I winced. The police!

If only.

Mom's car pulled up alongside me and stopped dead in the middle of the street. She rolled her window down and, staring straight ahead, said, "Get in the car."

Her voice was dull and even. Any emotion had been ironed out from her vocal cords.

I kept walking.

Bold move, I know, but it was my only chance at surviving the night.

Mom stepped out of the car, the engine still running. She was only a few steps behind me, but I didn't stop. Or turn. I just kept walking.

"I have been driving around all night looking for you." Her voice cut the dark. "There was no basketball game, so why don't you tell me where you've been for the last six hours? Or maybe you've got another fairy tale to share with me?"

I stopped walking and turned toward Mom for the first time. I couldn't see her face. She remained silhouetted by the headlights behind her.

I stormed past her. I just wanted to get in the car and go home.

Mom grabbed me by the shoulder and spun me around.

"Tell me, Spencer."

Her face was now illuminated by the headlights. Mascara streaked her cheeks, like tire marks skidded across her skin.

I got into the car.

Neither of us talked the whole ride home.

DODGEBALL FOR DUNCES

Where were the boys in blue?

The morning after our rampage, I expected to find the entire school cordoned off by yellow tape, and sniffing dogs searching for evidence of the delinquents responsible for what had to be a million dollars' worth of damage.

But nothing. The halls were spotless. The bathrooms were immaculate.

Like it had never happened.

Except for one telltale reminder. Our rebellious pièce de résistance.

Griz the Grizzly was still hanging from the basketball hoop, stuffed with funky gym uniforms—an inspired act of athletic taxidermy.

Simms was called over the intercom before the first bell rang: "Mr. Simms to the gymnasium, we have a busted pipe. Mr. Simms to the gymnasium . . ."

No busted pipe here. Just a bloated bearskin rug dangling from the rim for everybody in my first period gym class to see.

At first I figured I'd feel a swell of pride. But watching Mr. Simms set up his ladder suddenly made me feel ashamed. I found myself wanting to apologize.

"Who do you think did this?" I asked innocently.

"Got me." Simms shook his head as he cut Griz's limp body down. "Just another dumb prank."

Griz landed with a soft thud, in a heap of his own fur.

● ● ●

Almost twenty-four hours later, and the aroma of burned bacon wrapped in used diapers still lingered.

Coach Calhoon could've canceled Phys Ed—but nope:

Dodgeball must go on.

● ● ●

It was down to me and Martin Mendleson.

"Looks like it's just us," I said, hoping to break the ice. "May the best man get picked next to last."

"Stay away from me," Martin muttered.

"What? What did I do?"

"Pritchard grilled me all morning. He thinks I had something to do with yesterday."

"That sucks."

"Quit acting innocent. I told him it was someone else in Griz's costume. And everyone knows you were MIA during the pep rally—so if anybody gets blamed, it's bound to be you."

So much for solidarity.

But he had a point.

"Come on, ladies," Coach Calhoon barked. "We don't have all day!"

Coach had selected two captains while the rest of us filed in along the sidelines, waiting to hear our names called. The choice players were quickly divvied up:

Lisa Amazonian on one side.

Walter Goldmedal on the other.

Thomas Olympiad over here.

Jason Conquest over there.

You know the drill. Alpha-athletes first. Then the bench-warmers.

"You take him." Thomas nodded at me.

"No way I'm getting stuck with that freak," Lisa fired back. "You take him!"

"You can have them both!"

"Fine, fine." Lisa rolled his eyes. "We'll take . . ."

I held my breath.

This was it. The moment of truth. *Please don't let me be the last. . . .*

"Martin."

It's official. I'm the biggest loser in all of Greenfield Middle School.

"All right, then!" Coach Calhoon yelled. He blew the silver whistle noosed around his neck. "Let's play some dodgeball!"

Ten red rubber balls were lined up along the center mark. Players took their positions behind their team's end line, fifteen members on each side.

"The game's not over until only one team is left standing!"

Coach blew his whistle again, and heels skidded across the court as the players on each team raced to retrieve as many balls as possible.

In a breath, the air was full of red flashes.

There was a hiss of rushing rubber. Before he even knew what hit him—*Thwonk!*—Jason went down.

Another red mortar took out Walter directly on my right—*Thwonk!*

On my left, three teammates were sent to dodgeball heaven—*Thwonk! Thwonk! Thwonk!*

We were getting slaughtered and the game had barely even started.

I hadn't thrown a single shot yet, focusing on my *dodging* more than my *balling*. I felt like a ballerina plié-ing my way through a barrage of cannon fire.

"What're you doing, Pendleton!?" Coach Calhoon shrieked. "Get some action!"

"Doing my best, sir . . ."

Another comrade, Kerry Steib, was sent to an early grave next to me. My fallen brothers-and-sisters-in-arms gathered on the sidelines while I continued to escape impact.

"Pick up a ball, Pendleton!" Coach screamed.

"Working my way up to it, sir!"

There were only a few players left. Miraculously, I was still alive. Usually I'd be black and blue by the final whistle, but today I was ducking and covering like a pro.

Olympics, here I come. . . .

I was standing there, alone on the court, and then it struck me why.

Nobody had been aiming for me.

They're saving me for last.

The other squad formed a ring around me. It'd been a while since I'd boned up on the Phys Ed rules of engagement, but I was pretty positive this wasn't how you played dodgeball.

Not that Coach Calhoon seemed to mind. Quite the opposite. From the big grin spread across his face, I would've gone so far as to say he was enjoying himself.

"Looks like it's just you, Pendleton." Calhoon's chest swelled. "Let this be a lesson—*Don't you ever jerry-rig my gym with your stink bombs again.*"

My gym teacher was using the class to brandish his own vigilante justice.

There's no way this could've been aboveboard.

Or legal.

"One word of this to Pritchard and I could have you fired," I shot back.

"Who do you think Pritchard would listen to? It'd be your word against mine." Calhoon turned toward his werekids. "Ain't that right, team?"

Thomas grabbed a ball. Then Lisa. Even members of my own team picked one up and began bouncing their ammunition. The hollow *thwonk* of dribbled rubber reverberated through the gym like church bells before a funeral.

My funeral.

"Any last requests?" Thomas asked, ready to put me out of my misery.

"Tell my mother I loved her?"

"Say good-bye, *newbie*. . . ."

(Quick question: How long does one have to wait before he or she is officially no longer a newbie? Does it take a *newer* newbie to come in before the *older* newbie loses newbie status? Or is one cursed to be a newbie until the day one dies of a dodgeball-related death?)

Thomas brought his arm back, locked and loaded . . .

Only, the ball in his hand withered. The rotund rubber cannonball shriveled into an enormous dried cranberry.

"What the . . . ?" Thomas started.

"What are you all waiting for?" Coach Calhoon barked. "Finish him!"

Lisa reeled her arm back and let fly a streak of red rubber.

Good-bye, cruel gym class. . . .

But in mid-flight, the ball lost momentum. It veered off course and sank harmlessly to the floor, the air hissing out like an untied balloon.

Next thing you know, every ball was shriveling. No matter whose hands it was in.

Walter's ball.

Jason's ball.

One moment, the whole class was about to sacrifice me to the dodgeball gods—the next, their hands were clinching sagging red rubbery sacks.

It was Martin who first noticed the paper clip sticking out from his ball. He plucked it from the deflated rubber. "Where the heck did this come from?"

I didn't need a closer look to know it was a paper clip unfolded to a slender needle, weighted with a bulb of Scotch tape around its rear end.

"We're under attack!" Coach Calhoon blew his whistle, then hit the gymnasium floor. "Duck and cover! *Duck and cover!*"

Everyone was so busy watching him that no one noticed the shifting shadows beneath the bleachers. No one but me.

Between each row was an open slit, perfect for an attack. Just aim through one of the openings, fire at will, and take out an entire gym class's worth of dodgeballs.

So cool.

It amazed me how stealthy the Tribe could be, moving around

Greenfield without being noticed. They had mastered the art of covert classroom tactics and clandestine counterattacks.

Peashooter was right. They could do whatever they wanted.

Sign me up.

"Spencer Pendleton to the office, please." Pritchard's voice abruptly crackled out from over the intercom. "Spencer Pendleton to the office."

Just when I thought Pritchard had gone soft, it sounded like he wanted to pin the smoke-bomb attack on me after all.

"Catch you guys later," I called out to my classmates. "Better watch your balls. . . ."

A kid doesn't need a hall pass after an announcement like that.

Dead man walking.

THE OL'
ONE-TWO
SUCKER PUNCH

My eyes wandered around Pritchard's desk, taking an inventory of every stray pencil and loose sheet of paper.

No stapler this time. He must've attack-proofed just for me.

"I can explain," I started.

"Explain what?" Pritchard was acting all curious, like he had no idea what I could possibly be talking about.

Well—this is new.

There was a dinged-up book sitting on his desk. The cover was half torn, its pages curling into themselves.

"*The Catcher in the*—what?" I tried reading upside down.

"*Rye.*"

"Never heard of it."

"You wouldn't get your hands on this until high school," Pritchard said. "It's not on any seventh grade reading list, but you strike me as someone who reads a bit above his age level."

He pushed the tattered batch of pages across the desk.

"You brought me in . . . just to give me a book?"

Pritchard smirked. "Considering all the after-school detentions you're serving, you're going to have a lot of time on your hands. Might as well bring along something good to read."

"My punishment is to read a book?"

"Who says reading's a punishment?"

"Me."

"I devoured *Catcher* when I was your age. Finished it in less than two detentions, so I started reading it all over again from the beginning."

"I'm sorry . . . but did you say when *you* were in detention?"

Pritchard nodded.

Just what is he up to?

"So you didn't call me in to talk about yesterday's smoke-bombing?"

"I've got no proof you had anything to do with it—do I? Unless there's something you want to share with me. . . ."

"Nope." I shook my head. "And just so we're clear, this has nothing to do with any other hypothetical catastrophe that might have happened here recently?"

"Guess not." Pritchard leaned over his desk. "But the next time I call you to my office for something you've *hypothetically* not done, believe me, it won't be to borrow a book."

I took a quick puff from My Little Friend to ease my breathing.

"Go ahead." He nodded at the book between us. "Take my copy. But be careful. Read at your own risk. A book like that can turn your whole life upside down."

Pritchard had no idea how upside down my life already was.

Maybe this could turn it right-side up again.

• • •

I was late to Witherspoon's class, thanks to my heart-to-heart attack with Pritchard.

She made up for my tardiness when she asked me to stay after the bell.

Today's really not my day.

She still had a few weeks left wearing an eye patch, thanks to my pencil-harpooning. It was pink to match her outfit. She looked like a pastel pirate.

"As I'm sure you're well aware, Spencer," she started, "you've been here barely more than a month and already you've come perilously close to failing."

"I'm a fast worker," I said, staring at her injured eye.

"Keep it up and you'll be sitting at the same desk next year when you repeat my class."

Every last wisecrack withered on my lips, leaving my head a hollow husk.

"It's not like I *want* to stay a seventh grader forever. . . ."

"With the way you've been acting," she said, "I would've

believed you wanted to be held back until you turned thirty."

Like the Tribe: eternal middle schoolers.

"That's not what I want, Mrs. Witherspoon. Honest . . ."

"Oh—so you do know my name? How lovely. So tell me, Mr. Pencil Gun: Why should I believe a word you say?"

"Because . . ." I was at a loss for words. *"Just because?"*

Witherspoon pondered this for a bit. "What if I were to offer you a deal?"

"I'd take it."

"Don't you want to know what it is first?"

"No offense, ma'am, but if the alternative is repeating this class again next year, I'll pretty much do whatever it takes."

Like run from one end of the school to the other in nothing but my underwear. Or swallow broken glass. Or submit my body to science class for experimentation.

"Considering your oral report made such an impression on your classmates," she said, "I'd like you to spend the rest of the semester researching your Swanahanzi tribe."

The tribe I made up? The group of headhunters that never even existed?

That *tribe?*

"I want a full report on my desk before Christmas break," she continued. "Five pages—typed out, double-spaced—detailing the origins and rituals of your so-called *cannibals.*"

"Is it too late to negotiate the terms?"

"If you're resourceful enough to conjure up an entire tribe of fictitious anthropophagi off the top of your head, then taking a month to write a paper on them shouldn't be a problem."

"But . . . *how*? You know they don't actually exist."

"Then write about a tribe that *does*."

• • •

I took the long way to Mr. Rorshuck's class. What was the rush? I ended up wandering the empty halls wondering what I was going to write about for Witherspoon.

With each class I passed, I could hear the disembodied voice of the teacher inside droning on about math.

Science

History

English

A dozen decrepit subjects bleeding into the hall.

"Spencer . . ."

Is it just me—or did someone whisper my name? I didn't want to know.

"Spencer!"

There it was again.

I looked up—and sure enough, there was Peashooter, looking down at me from an opening in the ceiling. He whispered down. "Meet us in the gym tonight."

"I can't," I said, trying to keep my voice low. "I'm grounded."

"Did it sound like I was asking?"

Before I could respond, the familiar rattle of keys echoed through the hall. Mr. Simms was coming. I lowered my head as we passed each other.

"Who're you talking to?"

"Just myself."

"Sounds like you're giving yourself a pretty hard time."

"Nothing I can't handle," I said, turning just in time to collide with—"Mr. Rorshuck!"

"There you are, Mr. Pendleton. We were beginning to worry about you."

Simms would have to mop the sarcasm off the floor if Rorshuck kept this up.

"Tell me why you're not in my classroom right now?" he continued. "If I'm not mistaken, the bell rang twenty minutes ago. . . ."

"I was just talking with Mrs. Wither—"

"Do you have a hall pass?"

"No . . ."

"Wandering through the halls without a pass is a punishable offense."

"But I was talking to a *teacher*!"

"See me after school today, Mr. Pendleton. You and I can continue our conversation during detention."

I glared at Mr. Simms, hoping he'd throw me a lifeline. No such luck.

"But that's not fair—"

Rorshuck cut me off. "Two days of detention. Now get to my class before I make it three!"

It was official: *Worst Day Ever.*

I peered up to see if Peashooter was still there, listening in. The ceiling panel had been pushed back into place.

God—what I wouldn't give to be up there with the rest of the Tribe right now. I'd throw it all away just to be done with these teachers and their status quo.

I'd leave all this crap behind in a heartbeat.

No more me.

The end of Spence.

That got me thinking. . . .

Whoever Peashooter had been before forming the Tribe, that kid didn't exist anymore. None of them did.

As far as they were concerned, their former selves were dead to the world.

Nothing but ghosts now.

Then it hit me: Every ghost deserves a good story.

GHOST STORY NUMBER ONE: PEASHOOTER

Chosen Name: <u>Peashooter</u>
Given Name: <u>Unknown</u>
Area of Study: <u>English</u>
Weapon of Choice: <u>Bic dart gun</u>
Last seen: <u>Unknown</u>
Notes: <u>Ringleader. Well read.</u>

(The following segments are personal exchanges between individual Tribe members and the author. These interviews occurred in the field without the aid of a recording device, for fear of apprehension, scribbled down by the author as soon as humanly possible in hopes of retaining their accuracy.)

PEASHOOTER FIELD NOTES ENTRY #1:
LOCATION: BOILER ROOM
TIME: 10:00 P.M.

Peashooter possesses the strongest set of lungs of anyone I've ever met. One quick inhale is enough to power up his weapon of choice: a hollowed-out ballpoint pen.

To discharge his weapon, he grips the barrel of his Bic in his palm so that the nose is barely exposed, then brings his fist up to his mouth and simulates a cough. Before his victim has time to blink, he can fire off as many as five hand-made darts.

PEASHOOTER: Whenever Mr. Rorshuck turned his back, I'd fire off a quick spitball. SMACK! I'd hit him right in the neck. I was an academic assassin.
ME: Ever get caught?
PEASHOOTER: Once. Some sixth grader ratted me out. . . . Riley Callahan.

Peashooter pulls the paper-clip piercing from his septum and unfolds it in front of me. In seconds, he's holding a slender dart, ready for loading.

PEASHOOTER: Anyone who rats on the Tribe gets one of these in their eyeball.

I believed him.
Notice the threat subtext: Join us and we'll be the best friends you've ever had. Defy us and we'll be your worst nightmare.
Friends for life or foes forever . . .

PEASHOOTER FIELD NOTES ENTRY #2:
LOCATION: AFTER-SCHOOL DETENTION—DAY 8
TIME: 3:00 P.M.

As a student, Peashooter practically lived in detention. He was there so much his parents stopped expecting him home in the afternoons.

PEASHOOTER: I liked having the classroom all to myself. After school, when most kids had already left and nobody else was around—this place felt like it was all mine.

That's where Peashooter created his reading list:

Lord of the Flies, by William Golding.
White Fang, by Jack London.
The Call of the Wild, by London, too.
The Outsiders, by S. E. Hinton.
Watership Down, by Richard Adams.
The Adventures of Tom Sawyer, by Mark Twain.
The Art of War, by Sun Tzu.
Johnny Tremain, by Esther Forbes.
The Red Badge of Courage, by Stephen Crane.

"Reading" is putting it mildly. Peashooter ate these books up. As soon as he finished flipping through a book, he'd start over again.

And again.

He memorized passages. He underlined sections. He dog-eared pages.

PEASHOOTER: It felt like these books were written just for me. Like each author wanted to have a direct conversation with me and me only.

Peashooter thought he knew these books better than anyone else. Even his teachers. He felt he understood their <u>true</u> meaning.

Whenever he raised his hand in English class, Mrs. Royer would take a deep breath, bracing herself for a hearty dose of devil's advocacy.

PEASHOOTER: I'd question her on everything. No matter what the book, I'd always dispute her: How do you know that's true? How can you be so sure that's what Jack London was writing about? Even if I knew she was right, I'd still call her on it. Just for the challenge. Truth is, I was the only one in class who actually read the books, anyway. . . .

Peashooter was Royer's best student. Even if he was a pain in her butt.

PEASHOOTER FIELD NOTES ENTRY #3:
LOCATION: AFTER-SCHOOL DETENTION—DAY 10
TIME: 4:00 P.M.

For Peashooter, class was in session during detention. Not the other way around.

After a while, he couldn't help but feel bored by his regular school day. All six periods became speed bumps between him and his own personal lesson plan.

According to Peashooter, his teachers didn't teach middle school.

They taught day care.

PEASHOOTER: I couldn't wait for detention to start. All I wanted was to sit and read by myself.

ME: Why not just read at your house, then? If all you wanted was a little peace and quiet, couldn't you get that at home?

PEASHOOTER: Don't ever ask me about my home again. Got it?

The look in his eyes made his message loud and clear.

PEASHOOTER FIELD NOTES ENTRY #4:
LOCATION: AFTER-SCHOOL DETENTION–DAY 13
TIME: 3:00 P.M.

As soon as one sentence ran out, Peashooter made sure to wreak enough havoc to land him right back in detention.

PEASHOOTER: I'd spitball the principal if it got me an extra week. Solitary confinement was just what the doctor ordered.

It was on one of these quiet and confined afternoons that Peashooter considered the fiberglass panels over his head.

PEASHOOTER: It felt like the ceiling was calling me. . . .

He waited until the teacher on guard detail slipped out for a bathroom break. Alone, he stacked a bunch of encyclopedias on his desk, climbed up, pried apart the paneling, and peered in.
On the other side, he found three feet of crawl space between the classroom ceiling and the roof, a

cobwebbed hollow full of air-conditioning ducts and electrical wiring. The lower ceiling was nothing more than an aluminum grid held in place by a series of wires suspended from the upper ceiling. Each square grid held its own fiberglass tile.

The next day, when the teacher left the room, Peashooter actually climbed inside. He crawled around for a bit, testing his weight, making his way from one end of the classroom and back without falling through.

PEASHOOTER: The panels aren't strong, so it's best to crawl across the aluminum frame surrounding the tile. The trick is to evenly distribute your weight. You don't want to place all your heft on one portion of your body. You'll fall right through the ceiling. Crawl on your hands and knees.

On the third day, Peashooter climbed up and never came back. He slid the paneling back in place, sealing him in and officially cutting off his ties with the world down below.

PEASHOOTER: All I wanted were my books. It was the only part of my old life that mattered, so I took them with me. Everything else, I left behind.

ME: That teacher must've been surprised to return to an empty classroom.

PEASHOOTER: Whatever. I bet he was happy to be rid of me once and for all. I bet the whole school was.

ME: Ever think you'll go back?

PEASHOOTER: Go back where? Out there? With the rest of—who? You? Them? The Art of War says, "Know thy self, know thy enemy."

It should be noted that whenever Peashooter talks, it's a mash-up of books, most of which I'd never read. I imagine Peashooter hovering above everyone's head, reading to himself or listening to whatever lesson is happening below, soaking it in.

Talk about academic cannibalism.

PEASHOOTER: I don't belong out there anymore. None of us do.

ME: But it's just middle school. . . .

PEASHOOTER: It's a jungle.

POP QUIZ:
HALLWAY
HEADHUNTING

"Here at Greenfield there will neither be peace nor rest." Peashooter's voice echoed through the empty hallways. "Nor a moment's safety!"

I had no idea why I had been summoned.

All I knew was that I had snuck out of my house—just to sneak back into school.

Now, *that* was a first.

Having spent the majority of my middle school existence attempting to *break out* of school, never in a million years would I have imagined wanting to *break in*.

Mom was keeping a pretty close eye on me that night. She had already peeked her head into my bedroom three times, to make sure I wasn't up to anything.

"How's your homework coming?"

"Just reading."

"Oh yeah?" She perked up. This was the most we'd said to each other all day. "What're you reading?"

"A story called 'The Most Dangerous Game.'"

"What's it about?"

"This one guy hunts another guy in the jungle."

"Sounds interesting. Any good?"

"It's okay, I guess. . . . I'm only halfway through it."

"Anything exciting happen at school?"

If I'd told her I'd served yet another detention, she would have flayed me alive. "Nothing really. Hung out with some friends."

"Really?" She seemed pleased. "When can I meet these friends?"

"I'm on a trial basis with them right now. They want to see if I'm a good fit."

"Well . . . good luck, I guess. Is that the right thing to say?"

"Works for me."

"Don't stay up too late reading, Spence," she said as she closed the door. Through the paneling, I just barely heard her say, "Love you."

I had to wait until I was sure that she was asleep before I tiptoed down the stairs and slipped through the kitchen window. Then I hoofed the two miles back to Greenfield.

While I walked, I did a quick supply check:

Flashlight? *Check.*

My Little Friend? *Check.*

Cojones? *Well . . . I might've left those at home.*

I circled around the building twice before discovering a window in the industrial arts workshop that had been left open. I shimmied through, landing in a pile of sawdust.

Great. I stood up, coughing and completely covered in wood shavings.

Dusting myself, I heard faint rumblings farther off.

Voices.

Someone was shouting. I stepped into the hallway, and sure enough, it was Peashooter. I'd recognize his rally cry anywhere. It sounded like his voice was coming from the gym.

"You are savages! You know no law but the law of claw and fang!"

Someone else—Sporkboy, I bet—called back: "To the law of claw and fang!"

Slipping into the gym, I found the Tribe sitting within the center circle of the court. Each member had a javelin.

Peashooter stood above the rest—chest puffed, chin lifted—marching around the others in some fervent version of *Duck Duck Goose.*

"This is your introduction to the reign of primitive law," he bellowed. "The law of claw and fang!"

Sporkboy raised his fist into the air. Yardstick and Compass, too. Each one of them, save for Sully, had scribbled *CLAW* across the knuckles of their left hand and *FANG* over their right.

They roared—"Claw and fang!"

"Claw and fang!"

"Claw and fang!"

"Silence!" Peashooter had spotted me. "Look who finally made it."

Sully looked over first.

"Sorry I'm late. . . . What did I miss?"

"We've brought in new blood to strengthen our tribal line," Peashooter continued. "But first—the lamb must prove he's worthy of our ranks. He must earn his place among us, as we all did."

Just what is Peashooter getting at here?

"Ready for your first pop quiz, Spencer?"

"Uh . . . pop quiz?"

"Tonight we put your survival skills to the test."

"Survival skills? What's there to survive?"

"Life is for the strong," Peashooter thundered, *"to be lived by the strong, and, if need be, taken by the strong. The weak of the world were put here to give the strong pleasure. I am strong. Why should I not use my gift? If I wish to hunt, why should I not?"*

I recognized this.

"The Most Dangerous Game." He was quoting "The Most Dangerous Game"!

I'd just read that. I quoted right along with him: *". . . I hunt the scum of the earth."*

Peashooter flashed me his patented grin. "Guess somebody

did their homework after all. Sure hope you took notes."

"So . . . what am I supposed to do?"

"You've got to find a way out of the building—or your head will end up mounted to the boiler room wall."

Peashooter nodded to Sully.

"Thirty . . . twenty-nine . . . twenty-eight," her voice intoned. The Tribe all stood, one after the other, picking their javelins up from the floor.

Hold on a sec, I thought, kicking myself for not finishing my assignment. How exactly did "The Most Dangerous Game" end?

"Twenty-seven . . . twenty-six . . ."

And why is everybody else armed with track-and-field equipment?

"Twenty five . . . twenty four . . ."

This doesn't feel right, Spencer. Something's really wrong here. . . .

"Twenty-three . . ."

Run, Spence!

"Twenty-two . . ."

Now!

I booked it out of the gym and into the hallway. I could hear the numbers as they slipped away: "Twenty-one . . . twenty . . . nineteen . . ."

I kept the countdown going for myself, maintaining Sully's metronome pace just under my breath. "Eighteen . . . seventeen . . . sixteen . . ."

I had barely made it to the end of the hall before I'd reached the single digits—"Nineeightsevensixfivefourthreetwoone . . ."

A shrill cacophony of gym whistles pierced my ears.

The hunt was on.

$$\bullet \; \bullet \; \bullet$$

Let me take this opportunity to briefly explain the layout of Greenfield Middle School.

Picture an enormous bat.

Beginning with the two fanged flagpoles on the front lawn, Greenfield was designed to suck the very marrow from its students.

The administrative offices serve as its head. Once kids walk through the gaping maw of the main entrance, they are plunged into the central hallway. All of the administrative offices funnel through the gullet, from Pritchard's lair, to attendance, guidance, and the school nurse. From there, you reach the expansive quarters—spaces like the gymnasium, cafeteria, and library—all connected together at the building's core. Think of this area as the bat's torso.

The cafeteria is fittingly positioned around the stomach.

The library is the heart.

The gym? Let's consider that the part of the bat's anatomy where the sun doesn't shine.

But what Greenfield has most in common with the bloodthirsty *Desmodus rotundus* is the fact that—this building has wings.

Vast, academically segmented wings.

Outstretched at either side of the school's torso is an annex of twenty classrooms. Crescent-shaped, they curve inward as if in mid flap, ready to pluck up some poor unsuspecting student with their claws and fly away.

Math and sciences, along with several of our elective courses like industrial arts and home ec, are found within the left wing—while English and history, plus the auditorium and the orchestra room, are found on the right.

Whoever designed this building probably didn't take into account that this fat bat turns into a death trap at night. The school was cavernous enough during the day when the lights were on, but in the dark, without any windows, the halls felt more like century-old catacombs. And the lockers clustered together could have been tombs, for all I knew, each one containing the mummified remains of some sixth grader.

I could've sworn I heard a few bony fingers scraping across the other side of those tiny metal doors as I ran by.

Quit it, Spence. Keep a grip on that overactive imagination of yours!

•••

I headed for the right wing. There was an exit at the very tip.

I gripped my flashlight but kept it off. The light would have been a dead giveaway.

That meant running in the dark.

If I can just reach the end of the hall, I might have a chance at breaking out of the building before losing my head.

Just then—*whack!* A thump in the stomach. The impact sent me buckling over.

I briefly turned on my flashlight to see what it was.

A track hurdle.

I aimed my light farther down the hall.

Dozens of hurdles were lined up along the corridor.

As I stood there, my flashlight darting through the maze, I thought I heard footsteps. I snapped off the light and strained my ears.

Nothing. Everything was silent.

Hold it together. Keep quiet. They could be close.

No time to reach the exit.

I tried to open the nearest door. *Locked.*

So I tried the next. *Locked.*

Come on, come on!

Sweat started rolling down my brow, into my eyes. The salt stung.

This is not good. This isn't good at all.

One more door. I grabbed hold of the handle.

Please open please open please—

Unlocked!

I rushed into the pitch-black classroom and slammed the door behind me.

Quick. A barricade. I need a barricade!

The teacher's desk. *Perfect.* I pushed the desk against the door. The legs squealed over the linoleum—*instant giveaway.*

But I was safe. Better to be stuck in here with them out there.

All the windows in our classrooms, save for those in industrial arts, were hermetically sealed year-round, but I tried opening this one anyway.

No luck.

No way out.

No air.

A wave of light-headedness rushed over me, and I leaned against the bulletin board to keep myself from falling.

Quick: Huff a puff from My Little Friend.

I let myself slide to the floor and sat there trying to hold it together. I closed my eyes, slowly getting my breath back.

WHOOSH!—the air hissed by my shoulder.

I reached out and plucked a technical drawing instrument that had skewered the bulletin board.

Someone was in the room with me!

Looking up through the dim light, I could make out a ceiling panel that had been pushed back.

Oh no oh no oh no . . .

A shadow shifted across the room.

Compass. He scurried down an aisle of desks and disappeared.

I leapt to my feet and shoved the front row of desks together, boxing him in. Then I grabbed the nearest corner of the teacher's desk and yanked. The desk was too heavy to budge much, but it gave me just enough space to open the door and squeeze through.

But not before another compass buried itself into the door's wooden paneling.

"Whyah!" I blurted out as I toppled back into the hallway.

I shined my flashlight in front of me and charged every single blockade that stood between me and the exit.

A javelin struck a locker to my left. The rattle of metal reverberated through the hall.

"Yea-ah!"

Something grabbed my ankles.

One second I'm hightailing it down the hall, doing my best at half-blind hurdling—the next, my legs are tangled together.

"Whoa, whoa—"

Instantly cinched.

Face-plant.

Carpet burn.

My flashlight. What happened to my flashlight?

The beam rolled back and forth across the carpet before finally stopping on a pair of bare feet heading my way.

Yardstick.

I flipped over onto my back—and what did I find?

A jump rope with each end tied to a hacky sack for extra weight.

I kept kicking until the homemade bola started to slacken. Then I pulled my left foot out and stumbled back up.

This is all about pushing me down the hall. They're trying to corral me.

But to where?

Just get out of the building now, Spencer. Go, go, go!

I made a mad dash to the exit, and a wave of relief washed over me as I pushed the door. . . .

Only it wouldn't open.

The handle was padlocked and wrapped in chains.

I pushed again, harder. The chains rattled, but the door wouldn't budge.

I should have known: run down either wing and you hit an exit.

But if the exit is chained, you're trapped.

Like a rat.

Somebody blasted a whistle, but it was impossible to tell who it was or from where. It was immediately answered by a warble in the hall. That had to have been Sporkboy.

He was joined by another call, sounding like it had come from my left.

They were communicating with one another, telling each other where they were.

Then another call from behind . . . I think.

Three of them, and they were getting louder.

No. Not louder.

Nearer.

They were closing in.

"Kill the pig!"

"Cut his throat!"

"Spill his blood!"

I had to get past them.

I pressed my back against a row of lockers and started sidling along. I had only gone a few steps before the lockers ended and I bumped into a water fountain. I quickly ducked, balling myself up directly next to it, and prayed the Tribe hadn't noticed.

Maybe they hadn't seen me.

Maybe.

I heard the soft slap of footsteps patter by.

"Which way did he go?" one of them whispered.

"He was just here!"

"Well, find him!"

I waited until I knew they had walked a few steps past, then gave myself another second before bolting.

"There he goes!"

I picked up speed. They were right behind me—Yardstick and Compass. Sporkboy, too. His panting had a slight whistle to it.

If I could make it back to the main body of the building without getting speared, I could reach the front entrance.

One by one, the charge of bare feet behind me dwindled. I must have put some distance between me and the rest.

The central hallway was just ahead. All I had to do was take a quick turn and . . .

I skidded to a halt.

I was suddenly staring through the Y-shaped barrel of Sully's slingshot, aimed straight at my nose. She was biting down on the mouthpiece of her silver-rimmed whistle.

The air emptied from my lungs.

"That was close," I whispered. "I thought I was goner. We've got to get to the front entrance before—"

Sully didn't lower her arm.

"Sully . . . ?"

Her slingshot remained trained on me.

"Please?"

Sully blew into her whistle.

I was on my own.

I darted past her before she could fire. I heard the *CLINK!* of a coin hitting the wall just to my right, quickly followed by another.

There was no way I'd make it to the front entrance now.

I had to hide.

Somewhere no one would think to look for me. Somewhere nobody would be crazy enough to go.

A place so out there, no one would even conceive of it as a hiding spot.

There was only one place I could think of.

• • •

"Spencer." Sully's voice crackled over the intercom. "Come out, come out, wherever you are. . . ."

At least I knew she was in the main office.

Where the boys were—that was a totally different question.

Where was I?

Outside the cafeteria with a cluster of industrial-size rubber trash cans. Even when empty they smelled worse than death. We're talking half-eaten spaghetti that looked like shriveled earthworms, and coagulated soda cans with chunks of chewing gum stuck to the rims.

No one would ever, *ever* get inside one of these trash cans if they had the choice. The smell instantly set off my gag reflex, and I dry-heaved, *hee-hawing* like some colicky donkey.

It was too late to turn back now. I took another puff from My Little Friend, jumped in, and kneeled down.

Something runny started seeping into the knees of my jeans.

Please let that be soda.

I tried to hold my breath, but the smell was so strong. I didn't need to inhale for the nastiness to crawl inside my nostrils. It wriggled up my nose all on its own.

My asthma was eating away at my chest. No matter how many hits off my inhaler I took, I couldn't keep my lungs from burning.

Footsteps. I heard footsteps. They'd be right beside me any second now.

If I breathed through my mouth, my rasp would give me away—but if I breathed through my nose, I'd have to contend with an olfactory onslaught of rotten food.

"Where is he?" I heard one of them whisper.

"He's gotta be around here somewhere."

The longer I struggled to hold my breath, the more my lungs felt like they were flooding with battery acid. I'd black out before long.

Hold. Wait for it. Don't move until you know they're here.

Count of three:

One . . .

Two . . .

Three!

I jack-in-the-boxed out of the trash can and came face-to-face with Compass and Yardstick. I must've brought a waft of noxious aroma along with me, because both boys winced for a millisecond.

That was all I needed.

I grabbed the closest trash can and lifted it over my head and dumped it on Compass. The bin swallowed him up to his waist, and he started to shriek.

I quickly kicked the can, sending him toppling onto Yardstick. Both went down.

Run, Spencer. Run!

I had a good head start. I could make it to the front entrance. Sprinting down the hall, I nearly tripped over my own feet.

Almost there . . .

My rib cage had become a bony fist, tightening its grip around my lungs and squeezing.

So close. I could see the doors now. *So close so close so close.*

Another whistle. It sounded only a few steps away.

How could that be? How could they have caught up to me that quick?

Turning around, I found out.

The ergonomic swivel chairs from the administrative office were the only chairs in the building that had wheels. Spin the padded back of the chair to the front—and voilà: instant *chair*-iot.

The adjustable backrest becomes a defensive fortification. The metal legs branch out like a five-pointed starfish, so it's easy to plant your feet on the base and kick off—like a scooter.

It's one thing to see sweet apple-cheeked Mrs. Jarrow and a mothball-perfumed Mrs. Worsham pivoting behind the front desk in their chairs—answering phones, writing late passes, and typing up memos—but seeing the Tribe barrel down on me was something totally different.

Peashooter and Sporkboy piloted one chair-iot, while a pretty ticked off Compass and Yardstick shared their own. Peashooter and Yardstick were steering.

Sporkboy and Compass held separate ends of a volleyball net between them.

That net was meant for me.

"Take him down!" Peashooter shouted. "Throw it—*now*!"

Up ahead, I caught sight of Mr. Simms's mop and bucket. He had left it leaning against the wall just next to the entrance to the boys' bathroom.

If I could just . . .

I only have one chance.

Have to make it count.

I could sense Sporkboy and Compass reeling back—just a breath away from tossing the net. I leaned to my right, extending my hand as far as I could reach.

My fingers grazed the mop's handle. I could feel the coarse grain of the wood against my skin as it slid into the palm of my hand. I tightened my grip and yanked—only, the mop didn't leave the bucket.

Instead, it tipped over. Dirty, soapy water went cascading across the floor.

Yardstick didn't have enough time to steer clear of the bucket. Just as he brought his foot down for another kick, he stomped on the container, throwing him off-balance. Without anything else to hold on to, Yardstick grabbed Compass, sending the two toppling.

Their vacated chair-iot rolled down the hallway, completely empty.

Bingo. Free ride.

I launched the mop at Peashooter's head. He slammed on the brakes with his feet and ducked. That gave me just enough time to hop on board the chair-iot and shift gears.

"Get him! Get him!"

I turned to see Sporkboy and Peashooter behind me, spitting into their whistles.

"*Kill the pig!*" Sporkboy screamed.

"*Cut his throat!*" Peashooter yelled.

"*Spill his blood!*" they hollered together.

At the very end of the main hallway, right at the front entrance, stood Greenfield Middle School's glass-encased trophy shelf—filled with an entire league of brass-cast athletes frozen in playing positions. Even at night, the school left its lights on, to illuminate the lineup of miniature metal men perched on their pedestals.

Soccer players stuck mid-kick.

Baseball players fixed mid-swing.

As we barreled toward that shiny glass case, I couldn't help but imagine those miniature sluggers tightening their little fists around their tiny baseball bats, ready to defend themselves against our charge.

Or, at least, Sporkboy's and Peashooter's.

I leapt off my chair and fell, rolling across the floor.

"Watch out," Sporkboy squealed. "We're heading right for the—"

But it was too late.

Peashooter jumped off at the very last second. He tumbled onto the floor just a few feet away from me, leaving Sporkboy to careen into the case alone.

Glass shattered.

Trophies toppled.

Metallic athletes and shards showered Sporkboy. Most bounced off his belly, but a few fragments sank into his skin, bringing up blood in thin dribbles.

"Man down!" I yelled. "Man down!"

Peashooter rushed over and kneeled beside Sporkboy, who laid there, dazed, surrounded by little brass men with no faces.

"Did I . . . win a trophy?"

"Don't move him," I said, running up to them. From this close, I could see that Sporkboy's arms were laced in red ribbons. "We've got to take him to a doctor."

"No we don't," Peashooter countered.

"But he's bleeding!"

"Couple nicks," he insisted. "Take him to the nurse's office. Sully can patch him up."

"What about all that glass?"

"Just leave it."

"But they'll know we were here!"

By then, Yardstick and Compass had caught up to us.

"You okay?" Yardstick asked, his voice permeated with concern.

Peashooter motioned for the two of them to each grab an arm while he lifted a leg.

"Simms will clean it up," he said to me. "Now grab his other leg and help us get him to the nurse's."

"You can't expect Simms to pick up after you every time you leave a mess."

"Says who? *You?*"

"Um—can we discuss this some other time?" Sporkboy piped up. "I'm losing some blood here. . . ."

SPECTRAL
PROTECTION

Spencer?" Mom's voice struggled through the gelatinous muck of my sleep. "*Wake up, Spencer. Don't make me drag you out of bed. . . .*"

I had slipped back through the kitchen window less than an hour ago.

I could have slept for the next thirty days straight.

I had barely dozed for thirty minutes.

My body ached. Every muscle felt like moldy cold cuts left out in the sun. My bones may as well have been used matchsticks, burned to flimsy cinders.

"Please," I moaned from beneath the bedspread. "Just let me die in peace. . . ."

"You're leaving me with no choice here, hon."

Mom yanked the covers off and got her first whiff of

me—"Spencer! *What is that smell?* Have you been sleeping in a garbage can?"

Close.

•••

Three scorching-hot showers later and still I smelled like a Dumpster dweller. I felt as if I had peeled the outer two layers of my skin clear off, rinsing and scrubbing under a stream of blistering water. Now that I was rubbed raw, I looked like a piglet. Completely pink.

And yet the decrepit bouquet from that trash can insisted on clinging to me.

The warning bell to first period had already rung by the time Mom dropped me off at school, the car windows rolled down for the whole ride.

I shuffled into the boys' room for one last rinse before subjecting my fellow classmates to my special brand of B.O., praying I could at least eradicate the soda scum from under my fingernails.

"There he is." Leaning against the sink, as if he'd been waiting for me, was none other than Riley Callahan. "We were getting worried you were skipping."

I turned around, ready to book it out of the bathroom—only to find two of his cloned cronies popping out of the stalls. Each grabbed an arm. One lifted his foot and drove his heel into my knee pit. My leg abruptly flexed forward, sending me down to the floor. Both knees slammed against the tiles. The pain rang through my body. It felt like my patellas had exploded.

With both arms still in their grip, I must've looked like a bird trying to flap away.

"Riley," I managed to say, "haven't you learned anything from our last few run-ins?"

"What can you do to me? Sure seems like I've got the upper hand now."

"Don't you get it? You've got to stop. . . ."

"Or else—what? You're going to mousetrap me in the mouth again?"

"I'm just trying to protect you!"

"You call squirting me in the face with pepper spray *protection*?"

"It was asthma medicine, but whatever . . ."

"You always have an answer for everything, don't you?" Riley muttered. "You just have to get the last word in?"

"Never been a big believer in the whole *silence is golden* thing. . . ."

"Since you don't know how to shut up, I think it's time someone taught you."

The second bell rang.

"Hurry!" Cro-Magnon Crony #1 said. "I can't be late for class. . . ."

"Can it," Riley said as he reached into the urinal with his

bare hand, pulled out the toilet cake, and held the pink puck up to my face.

I tried to free myself, yanking both arms until I thought they'd pop from their sockets—but it was no use.

"What are you doing?" I asked.

"Me? *I'm* not doing anything." He brought the puck up even closer. "*You*, on the other hand, missed breakfast."

Cro-Magnon Crony #2 chuckled.

"*Wait*," I yelled. "Can't we just settle this like mature young adults? You stay on your side of the hallway from now on and I'll stay on mine?"

"Open wide. . . ."

I cricked my neck back as far as I could, facing the ceiling. *"Heeeeeelp!"*

Cro-Magnon Crony #1 wrapped his sweaty palm across my mouth.

"Move your hand," Riley ordered.

"But what if somebody hears him?" Cro-Mag asked.

"This will shut him up. . . ."

As soon as my mouth was free, I started pleading with the ceiling again. "I could use a little help here!"

"You don't have any friends at this school," Riley snorted. "Unless you've made up some imaginary pals to play with?"

"Something like that . . ."

"So where are they now?"

"That's a very good question."

I knew this was a long shot, but either the Tribe would come to my rescue, or I was chowing down on a urinal cake.

"Somebody! Anybody? *Pleeeeaaase!*"

I'm going to take the next three seconds of my life and press the SLOW-MO button for a little play-by-play:

SECOND ONE:

Cro-Mag Crony #1 was airborne in a breath. Just when he was about to fall face-forward—his feet flipped, turning his entire body upside down.

SECOND TWO:

Cro-Mag Crony #2 let go of my arm. He was about to make a break for the door, but suddenly he found himself flopping through the air alongside his friend.

SECOND THREE:

I saw Riley look down at his feet.

So I looked down at Riley's feet.

A lasso of jump ropes lay open and loose around his tennis shoes. Riley didn't have enough time to turn and see where the other end of the tether went, but I could make out the length of yellow cord reaching up into the rafters of the bathroom ceiling.

Yardstick is one heck of an engineer.

In one swift *swish*, the jump rope cinched itself around Riley's ankles and launched him off the floor.

He let go of the urinal cake, and it splattered across the floor.

"It's been good hanging out with you guys," I said, pinching the puck between my fingers. "We should do this again."

I leaned into Riley's face and brought the cake up to his lips. "Now *you* open wide. . . ."

Just as I was about to score a goal and ram that pink puck past his teeth, Riley shut his eyes. "Please," he whimpered. "Don't!"

Wait a minute. What am I doing?

I took a step back, dropping the urinal cake to the floor.

Just who is the bully here?

"Let's get you down before somebody—"

Peashooter dropped from the ceiling.

Yardstick and Compass followed, climbing down into the stalls.

Before Riley or either of his clones could spin around and see who had just joined us, Compass and Yardstick slipped sweaty headbands over their eyes, blindfolding them.

"What are you doing?" I asked.

Peashooter stormed up to me. "Unfinished business."

• • •

Riley made his grand entrance into the girls' locker room strapped to one of the office rolling chairs. He had been stripped down and blindfolded. His mouth was covered with duct tape, and he was now wearing nothing but a pair of girl's underwear.

Written in Sharpie marker across his chest, along his arms and legs, was: *Sticks and stones may break my bones but words will always hurt me.*

A knot had formed in my stomach before Peashooter and Yardstick gave Riley the ol' heave-ho into the locker room.

"Are you sure this is a good idea?"

"This is how we deal with bullies," Peashooter whispered. "After this, Riley won't be bothering you—or anyone else—ever again."

Bullying the bullies.

Interesting tactic.

On a silently mouthed count of three, Peashooter and Yardstick shoved Riley inside. The two slipped under the bleachers before the first cry of surprise.

"Oh my God—*look!*"

Why it hadn't dawned on me to bolt is beyond me.

"Is that . . . *Riley Callahan?*"

The moment his name was uttered out loud, the stunned silence that had overtaken the girls quickly shifted into something much more malevolent.

"It is! It *totally* is!"

One girl laughed. Then another. The more voices that added to the cackling, the louder the sound intensified—until it sounded wretched.

Inhuman.

Those girls transformed into a horde of werekids, turning on one of their own.

That's when I ran.

As much as I thought I wouldn't mind Riley getting a little taste of tribal comeuppance, I felt like I had abandoned him to be torn to pieces by that rabid pack.

• • •

My name was on the lips of a few too many students that day.

Boy, were my ears burning.

When Coach Calhoon pulled the gag out from Riley's mouth, the finger-pointing commenced: "It was Spencer Pendleton!" Riley cried. "He did this!"

When Mr. Simms was called to fix a "busted pipe" in the boys' bathroom, he discovered Callahan's cronies dangling from the ceiling instead: "Spencer Pendleton sneak-attacked us!"

When Pritchard called me into his office to hear my side of the story, he didn't say anything for the longest time. Jaw clenched.

I couldn't tell if he expected me to speak first, so I kept quiet.

He finally broke the silence. "You're here so much I should start charging you rent."

"Maybe you just enjoy my company, sir?"

"Do you always have a witty comeback? Or do you ever bite your tongue?"

"I've bitten my tongue plenty of times. You'd think I wouldn't have any tongue left by now. . . ."

"Greenfield has gone through an earthquake since you arrived," he said. "Damaged property. Broken trophy case. Stolen school supplies. Misplaced equipment. Smoke bombs. *Vandalism*. And now this incident with Riley and his friends!"

"But I haven't done anything!"

Technically speaking, it was the truth.

"I'm not an idiot, Spencer. I know it's you. I may not be able to prove every single last act of sabotage yet, but a student saw you running from the gym today."

"Okay, yes, I was there. But it wasn't me, I swear."

"Then who was it?"

I stopped myself from saying anything more. The walls had eyes.

More like the ceiling had ears.

"Consider this strike one." Pritchard sighed. "Three strikes and you're out, Spencer—and I do mean *out*. Out of my school. For good."

I looked up at him, locking on to his eyes.

"You're staying after school today for detention."

"What if I'm already serving a detention for Mr. Rorshuck?"

"We'll just have to add on another one," he said, shaking his head. "But from the moment you step into this building, there will be eyes on you. *Twenty-four/seven!*"

His weren't the only ones. . . .

"It's a deal, Jim," I said. "You won't be sorry, I promise."

"Please don't call me Jim."

GHOST STORY NUMBER TWO: YARDSTICK

Chosen Name: <u>Yardstick</u>
Given Name: <u>Jack Cumberland</u>
Area of Study: <u>Mathematics, Engineering</u>
Weapon of Choice: <u>Yardstick spear,</u>
<u>Javelin harpoon, Magic tricks.</u>
Last seen: <u>6th grade</u>
Notes: <u>Shy. Speaks only when spoken to. Genius engineer.</u>

YARDSTICK FIELD NOTES ENTRY #1:
LOCATION: AUDITORIUM
TIME: THIRD PERIOD. 10:30 A.M.

Every year, Greenfield Middle School holds its annual talent show.

YARDSTICK: Stepping on stage before the whole school is just about the scariest thing I've ever done. I'll never do anything like that again.

His shyness was so out of sync with his physique. Yardstick had a solid six or seven inches over the average student—but his voice was barely there. I had to lean in to hear what he was saying.
His yearbook photo could hardly contain him.

The photographer couldn't fit his head in the frame without pulling the camera back—and <u>still</u> the top of his head was cropped off.

It may have said his name was Jack Cumberland in the yearbook, but his classmates called him <u>Scarecrow</u>.

<u>Skyscraper</u>

<u>Flagpole</u>

<u>Air Control</u>

<u>Elevator Shaft</u>

He was in the sixth grade when he disappeared, soon after what happened in the talent show.

He told me his story while we were watching this year's parade of untalent, from the auditorium rafters. We'd hidden ourselves along the light grid directly above a steady stream of crappy song-and-dancers, crappy rappers, and crappy stand-up comedians.

At the moment, Yardstick had a solid rope of phlegm slithering down his lips. He slurped the loogie back into his mouth and swallowed.

YARDSTICK: The longest I've ever gone is about a foot.

ME: Was that your talent? Loogie yo-yo?

YARDSTICK: Nope.

ME: What, then?

YARDSTICK: Magic.

I thought he was kidding at first, so I laughed.

Bad move on my part.

I saw him wince, just the slightest pinch in the corner of his eyes, and I realized that he was one hundred percent <u>not</u> joking.

ME: Sorry. I didn't mean to laugh.
YARDSTICK: It's okay. I'm over it now.
ME: You sure?
YARDSTICK: Like Peashooter says, "Speak softly and carry a big yardstick."

I'm pretty sure that's not what President Teddy Roosevelt said when he originally said it, but why quibble?

This was the most Yardstick and I had ever talked to each other. In fact, it was the most I'd ever heard him say in one sitting—<u>period</u>.

Yardstick peered down at Sarah Haversand attempting to do an interpretive dance routine. He summoned as much phlegm from his chest as his lungs would allow, a quart at least, and let the saliva ooze from his mouth.

Six inches and counting . . .

Seven inches and counting . . .

Eight inches and counting . . .

Nine—

The tendril snapped. The loogie took a dive straight down, smacking Sarah directly on the head. She brought her hand up and patted the dampness on her scalp, only to look up toward the rafters, eyes wide in horror, and shriek.

She probably thought a pigeon just pooped on her head.

YARDSTICK: We better book it.
ME: Good idea.

YARDSTICK FIELD NOTES ENTRY #2:
LOCATION: UNDER THE BLEACHERS
TIME: THIRD PERIOD. 11:00 A.M.

Before his big night, Yardstick's mom had helped him into his father's tuxedo from some long-gone wedding. It was too short in the sleeves—which was no good. If his limbs poked out from his miniature tuxedo, he would've revealed the ingenious pulley system underneath.

YARDSTICK: Magic is really just engineering. The hand's always got to be quicker than the eye, so I designed this hidden quick-draw rig.
ME: Hidden what?

YARDSTICK: All you need is some Velcro, a drawer slide, some wire and tubes—and presto! You've got your own concealed pigeon-release rig.

Yardstick couldn't afford a dove—so he had to spend an entire afternoon at the park, struggling to catch a pigeon with his bare hands.

ME: You had a pigeon stuffed under your tux the whole time?
YARDSTICK: I should've figured out a better ventilation system.

When Yardstick took to the stage, the audience could see his sixth-grade scarecrow legs trembling.

YARDSTICK: I felt like my heart was gonna bust right out of my rib cage. I'd never been so nervous in all of my life.

He'd spent weeks leading up to the show, practicing. Perfecting his approach.
Rehearsing the pigeon trick over and over again until he knew the routine inside and out.
The judges were teachers. Mr. Fitzpatrick. Mrs. Witherspoon. Mrs. Royer. Mr. Rorshuck. They all sat

stone-faced in the front row, watching Yardstick pull out a never-ending noose of handkerchiefs from his tux.

YARDSTICK: I could feel the sweat soaking through my clothes. Like I was drowning inside my tux.

Not to mention his poor pigeon.
When it was time for his grand finale, the trick that would really wow the crowd, what Yardstick didn't realize was that his feathered assistant had already suffocated inside his armpit.

YARDSTICK: The mechanics of the trick itself worked perfectly. I had constructed this trigger system where all I needed to do was squeeze a key ring in my fist, setting off the drawer slide down the length of my arm and releasing the pigeon into the air.
ME: But . . . ?
YARDSTICK: But when the pigeon popped out of my sleeve, it had already kicked the bucket.

Instead of that bird soaring over everybody's heads, an explosion of feathers and blood splattered across the entire front row. The body of that feathered projectile shot directly into the face of one particular student.

Guess who?

Riley Callahan. <u>Pow!</u> Pigeoned right in the kisser.

Nobody clapped. Everybody screamed.

Yardstick was too afraid to bow. He ran offstage, all the way home.

YARDSTICK: All I wanted was for everyone to leave me alone.

Especially Riley and his cronies.

"Beanpole! How's the magic act? Learn any new stupid tricks?"

"Whatcha gonna do, Scarecrow? Pull a dead rabbit outta your butt?"

"Skyscraper! How's it feel to have the whole school hate you?"

The one magic trick he wished he'd done that night was disappear.

So, finally—he did.

One day, Yardstick stopped showing up to classes. His desk sat empty. His locker unopened. His library books unreturned.

Now you see him, now you don't.

<u>Poof.</u>

THE LAW
OF CLAW
AND FANG

All of you are consumed with a desire to extend the glory of the Tribe!" Peashooter addressed us from within the bowels of the boiler room.

With detention done for the day, I had just enough time to slip into the basement for a quick visit before heading home.

Now I found myself standing at attention as Peashooter marched past, inspecting each member one by one. The acne on Compass's face seemed to catch fire in proximity to his leader. Yardstick might as well have grown an extra six inches when he walked by.

Sporkboy's arms were mummified in bandages. On each of his round, apple cheeks were a pair of Band-Aids intersecting in the middle to form an X.

After he'd crashed headfirst into the trophy case, I would have expected him to sit the next few nights out. But, nope—here he was, standing in formation among the rest and sucking on a lollipop, hungry for whatever Peashooter had up his sleeve.

Talk about team spirit.

"You long to humiliate those arrogant students who dared make fun of us!"

Sully was leaning against a pipe. She glanced over at me and rolled her eyes behind Peashooter's back, as if to say, *Can you believe this guy?*

I couldn't help but laugh a little. A giggle slipped out before I could swallow it down.

Peashooter stopped in front of me. I could read: *FEAR* across one fist. Over the knuckles of the other, it said: *LOATH*.

"All of you wish to be able to say with pride . . ." he brayed, straight into my face, "I was with the victorious army of the Tribe!"

Peashooter's demagoguing monologues needed footnotes.

His speech came straight from world history that morning.

Forget about dealing with Napoleon Bonaparte in class.

I had Peashooter the Awesome.

"I don't mean to overstep my jurisdiction here," I piped up. "But I'm not so sure that's exactly what Napoleon had in mind when he said that. . . ."

Peashooter did a double take.

"Since when did you start paying attention in history?"

"As far as short French generals go," I said, "I'll admit I'm no pro. But I'm pretty positive Napoleon wasn't talking about getting back at his classmates for teasing him. . . ."

I'm sorry, Peashooter, but you're no Bonaparte.

Whenever Compass got angry, fresh fields of whiteheads sprouted across his cheeks. "You've got a lot of nerve contradicting our captain."

"All I'm saying is—Peashooter's twisting Napoleon's words around. If you listen to the whole speech, you'd know he makes his soldiers promise to *respect* their enemy."

"*Respect?*" Compass huffed. "Our enemies don't deserve our *respect.*"

"Napoleon even says to the people he was about to conquer," I continued, "*We are waging a war as generous enemies, and we wish only to crush the tyrants who enslave you.* While *you* just want to get back at everybody because some students made fun of you a long time ago."

Peashooter pulled out that grin of his. But this time, I could see his eyes slightly tightening.

I'd hit a nerve.

"Sorry, Spence," he said. "Stick with your fibbing. Leave history to me, okay?"

"Spencer's got a point," Sully spoke up.

Didn't see that coming. Nobody did. Not even Peashooter.

We all stared at her.

"It's true, isn't it?" she asked. "You're talking about revenge."

Peashooter turned back to me. He didn't look all too happy.

I think this boat just got rocked a bit. . . .

• • •

Witherspoontificate kick-started our class the following morning with a discussion on the decline of Napoleon.

"What could've caused the downfall of this once-mighty emperor?" she asked. "Can anybody think of an example of what lead to Napoleon's demise?"

Sarah Haversand's hand shot up. "The invasion of Russia?"

"Yes—the disastrous Russian invasion in 1812. What else? Anyone have any thoughts?"

I raised my hand.

That's right: *I actually raised my hand.*

"Spencer? You have something constructive to contribute?"

"Seems to me like he got a little carried away," I said.

"What do you mean by that?"

"Maybe he wore out his welcome and should've called it quits while he was ahead and before somebody else overthrew him and sent him and his men to juvie hall for the rest of their lives. . . ."

"That's . . . *mostly* true. Napoleon was overextending his army because of his ambition to control more and more of the European continent. Sometimes your desire to control can lead to your own defeat."

I hoped somebody up above was listening.

"Mr. Simms." Pritchard's voice sputtered out from the intercom. "Please come to the boys' bathroom. We have another busted pipe. . . ."

I raised my hand again.

"Something else, Mr. Pendleton?"

"May I have a pass to the bathroom, please?"

• • •

I finally broke the administration's code.

Took you long enough, Spence.

Whenever Pritchard mentioned a "busted pipe" over the intercom, it meant Mr. Simms had to slog through the aftermath of another tribal act of sabotage.

Talk about employee of the month.

Peashooter had pilfered the master list of locker combinations from the office, then gutted the lockers and stuffed their contents down the toilets.

Homework assignments. Notes from class. Graded test papers.

All soaked.

"Any idea who did this?" I asked.

Mr. Simms glanced at me, then turned back toward the mess.

"Bathroom's out of order," he said. "Best you use another one."

"Mind if I help?"

"Don't you have some class to go to?"

I nodded. "Probably."

"Suit yourself."

Mr. Simms got to work on mopping up the flood of toilet water.

I picked up a sheet of loose-leaf paper floating on the floor, the ink bleeding across the page. "Do you always clean up after them?"

"I don't know what you're talking about. . . ."

"You know *exactly* what I'm talking about."

He turned around and looked me dead in the eyes. "What if I do?"

"So all this time I've been saying there's a tribe of kids running around school and you acted like you didn't believe me, like I was crazy, *you knew they were here*?"

Simms went back to his mopping without saying another word.

"Who else knows about them?"

"Just us, far as I can tell," he admitted. "That's probably how they want to keep it."

"Are you gonna let them get away with this?" I whispered, wondering if there were eyes staring down at us from the ceiling.

"You mean rat them out?" Mr. Simms huffed. "Who'd believe me?"

I knew how he felt.

He checked to see if the coast was clear, then whispered, "I hear they've asked you to join."

"How do you know that?"

"Just because I'm a janitor doesn't mean I don't see what's going on." He sounded a little offended. "My advice? Not that you asked."

"What?"

"Better know what you're getting yourself into."

• • •

Mrs. Royer started off our English class by scribbling *THE CALL OF THE WILD* BY JACK LONDON across the blackboard.

"*Here was neither peace, nor rest, nor a moment's safety,*" she read from her book. "*All was confusion and action, and every moment life and limb were in peril . . .*"

I peered up toward the ceiling, not surprised to see the fiberglass panel pulled back.

Of course.

For the last part of the passage, Mrs. Royer placed her copy down on her knee and looked out at the class, reciting the rest by heart. "*They were savages, all of them, who knew no law but the law of . . .*"

I recited right along with her: ". . . *Claw and fang.*"

"Spencer!" Mrs. Royer's eyes widened. "I'm impressed. You're one of only two students to have read this book before I assigned it in class."

"Who was the first?"

Of course I knew who it was.

"You wouldn't know him. . . . He wasn't here for long."

"What was his name?"

All I needed was to hear her say Peashooter's true name.

Research for Operation: Tribal Identity Retrieval had hit a brick wall with him, and I was desperate to know.

The other members of the Tribe had been a cinch to pinpoint. It had taken a little sifting through the yearbooks in the library, sure—but eventually I'd stumbled upon their pictures.

Sporkboy, Compass, Yardstick.

Even Sully.

I had unearthed photographs of their former sixth-, seventh-, and eighth-grade selves. Dressed in regular clothes. No arsenals strapped to their chests.

Not Peashooter, though. No photos. No records of his middle-school existence whatsoever.

Mrs. Royer swallowed. Her lips parted. She took in a quick breath:

"His name was—"

Bells shattered the classroom.

The fire alarm. Somebody had pulled the fire alarm.

I'll give you one guess who.

"Well, everybody," Mrs. Royer called out over the clamor, "you know the drill. Out into the parking lot!"

Students were herded through the hallway. I straggled at the back of the line.

Passing the boys' room, I heard something inside.

An oink.

Could've been my imagination—but I stepped inside. Seemed empty. The doors to each stall were shut.

Another oink.

"Who's there?"

I walked over to the first stall and pushed it open. Nothing behind door number one.

"Sully—that you?"

Opening the middle stall door, I suddenly came face-to-face with Sporkboy.

Guess I should've gone with door number three.

His face was masked with the kind of hairnet that the cafeteria ladies wear.

He was brandishing corn dog nunchucks.

I repeat: Corn dog. *Nunchucks.*

As in, Sporkboy had taken two frozen corn dogs from the cafeteria deep freeze and tied them together with a shoestring. He swung them through the air in total ninja fashion. Those petrified hot dogs blurred into a battered haze until one of them landed directly on my shoulder. The cold sting rang through my bones.

"*Ow!*"

"That's from Peashooter," he said, jabbing me in the chest with his corn dogs. "Stop sniffing around."

"How do you keep those things so frozen?" I rubbed my shoulder.

"Liquid nitrogen from the science lab," Sporkboy said. "Compass came up with it. It freezes things superfast and for hours."

"Compass has way too much time on his hands."

"Follow me," Sporkboy said, dragging me out of the bathroom. I spotted the graffiti scrawled across his arm: *MODEL STUDENT*. "We don't have much time."

"Wait—where are we going?"

GHOST STORY NUMBER THREE: SPORKBOY

Chosen Name: <u>Sporkboy</u>
Given Name: <u>Benjamin Greenwood</u>
Area of Study: <u>Wild-card, Arts and Crafts</u>
Weapon of Choice: <u>Spork-daggers, natural gas,</u>
<u>mascot-Kevlar, penny-roll mace</u>
Last seen: <u>6th grade</u>
Notes: <u>Off his rocker. Daredevil. Wants to impress the rest.</u>

SPORKBOY FIELD NOTES ENTRY #1:
LOCATION: CAFETERIA
TIME: FOURTH PERIOD. 11:20 A.M.

Sporkboy hefted a tub of dehydrated mashed potatoes across the cafeteria floor. He poured a gallon of water into the vat of desiccated flakes, gleefully stirring up his caldron full of instant spuds with a ruler.

SPORKBOY: We don't use our old names anymore. We're new people now, so we need new names.
ME: New? New how?
SPORKBOY: Nobody wants to be who they were. Now we can be whoever we want to be.

His name used to be Benjamin.

Benjamin Greenwood.

I first found his picture after flipping through three years' worth of Greenfield Middle School yearbooks. Even though the picture was in black and white, I could totally tell that was Sporkboy's carroty-red curly hair. Those were Sporkboy's freckles spread all over his chubby cheeks.

Werekids would pick on him because of his weight.

SPORKBOY: I'd be walking down the hall, just trying to get to class, when somebody would come up and punch me in the gut.

He got called all kinds of names:

Lard Bucket

Garbage Disposal

Barf Bag

Benjamin was in the sixth grade when he disappeared. One day he was getting teased in English class—the next, his desk was just empty.

When I pressed him to tell me why he'd left everything behind—his family, his friends, his whole life—he grinned so wide his cheeks pinched his eyes until I couldn't see them anymore.

SPORKBOY: I found my real friends.

ME: And nobody picks on you anymore?

SPORKBOY: Peashooter says, "When people tease you, it's only because they're afraid of something they sense in you. Something they don't understand. The only way they know how to deal with it is to make fun of it. That's just because they're scared."

ME: Peashooter sure has a lot to say, doesn't he?

SPORKBOY: Peashooter always says, "The more you know, the more havoc you can wreak."

ME: He really says that?

SPORKBOY: All the time. He says, "Limited minds, limited havoc. Bigger minds, bigger havoc!"

ME: Well . . . how about you? What do you say?

SPORKBOY: What do you mean? Whatever Peashooter says, goes. That's the law of claw and fang.

So much for independent thought.

ME: So . . . what's with all the potatoes?

SPORKBOY: You'll see. "Double, double, toil and trouble . . ."

SPORKBOY FIELD NOTES ENTRY #2:
LOCATION: BOYS' BATHROOM
TIME: FOURTH PERIOD. 11:24 A.M.

It took some prying, but Sporkboy eventually told me what his last straw was.
Corn Dog Day.
Benjamin had sat down in the cafeteria, when some kid from class slid into the seat next to his.
It was none other than Riley Callahan.

SPORKBOY: Nobody ever sat at a table with me. Not on purpose. Certainly not Riley.

Benjamin had a rep for doing whatever people dared him to.
If you dared him to chew an old wad of bubble gum scraped off the underbelly of his desk—he'd do it.
If you dared him to pick up a fresh steaming dog turd with his bare hand—chances are, he'd do that too.
He and his pals had made a bet that Sporkboy couldn't eat ten corn dogs before the bell rang.
Ten corn dogs in less than ten minutes.
One corn dog per minute.

SPORKBOY: Here was Riley, this upper-tier, in-crowd

guy who acted like I didn't exist most days, daring me to dig in. . . .

All the other kids circled around the table while he chowed down, chanting out his name: "Benji! Benji! Benji!"
He chewed through his fifth corn dog.
His sixth corn dog.
His seventh.

SPORKBOY: The first few corn dogs went down okay. But then my throat started getting dry. By the time I got to number eight, I couldn't swallow anymore. The cornmeal mush started sticking in my throat. . . . It just wouldn't go down.

Rather than realize Benjamin wasn't capable of swallowing, Riley took the palm of his hand and pushed the tail end of corn dog number eight into his mouth.
He literally tried to <u>shove</u> it down Benjamin's throat.
The stick running through the middle of the corn dog slid through the meat and stabbed Benjamin in the back of his mouth.

SPORKBOY: It tapped at my gag reflex like he was pushing my upchuck button.

He brought up seven and a half corn dogs.

SPORKBOY: I puked all over Riley.

The entire cafeteria echoed in laughter. The sound still reverberated in Sporkboy's memory.
He told me he'd never eat another corn dog again.

SPORKBOY: Food with concealed weapons is a dangerous endeavor, you know?

SPORKBOY FIELD NOTES ENTRY #3:
LOCATION: CAFETERIA
TIME: LUNCH PERIOD. 11:45 A.M.

"Mr. Simms." Assistant Principal Pritchard's voice cut through the hallway as students started filing their way back inside the building. "Please come to the cafeteria. We have a busted pipe. . . ."
Not a busted pipe—but a bust of Riley Callahan rendered in mashed potatoes with a half dozen bread-battered hot dogs stuffed down his throat.
The likeness was quite striking.
A crowd had gathered around the cafeteria doors to marvel at Sporkboy's masterpiece.
Today was Corn Dog Day.

POP QUIZ: WELCOME TO BLUNDERDOME

Friday night. Time to roam through the mall with my pals or catch a movie at the multiplex with my girlfriend.

Hardly.

Try, sneaking back into school.

There had been a note waiting for me in my locker after fifth period. It was in Sully's handwriting:

Meet me in the science lab tonight.

But when I slipped into the lab, it wasn't Sully who was waiting for me.

I found Peashooter and Compass instead. Compass was carrying a pillowcase with something heavy inside.

"What's going on? Where's Sully?"

"Yeah, sorry about that," Peashooter said. "She asked if we'd come pick you up."

Suspicion quickly took over.

"You got her to write that note, didn't you?"

Peashooter shrugged his shoulders. His patented grin crept out across his lips. He had tagged his arm with *LOST BOY.*

Why was I here?

Compass reached into the pillowcase and pulled out a jar with some kind of clear fluid sloshing around.

"Here," he said, holding the empty sack up to me. "Slip this on."

"You can't be serious. I'm a guy with *asthma*."

"One drop of this stuff and—*poof.*" Compass swirled the contents of the jar. "Out cold. I hope I got the recipe right. Haven't tested it out on a human subject yet."

"Yet?"

Peashooter slipped the pillowcase over my head, and something wet dripped across my forehead.

"Deep breaths," Compass said as the unexpected smell of Mentho-Lyptus seeped through the cotton.

I tried to fight, but my limbs suddenly felt rubbery.

"Maybe you should give him more." Peashooter's voice sounded like it sank an octave with each word. "Just to be sure."

My head got heavy. My neck couldn't hold it up.

Anybody got a pillow?

• • •

I woke to a mechanical hum. At least that's how it sounded from under the pillowcase. A full-on migraine pounded against my eardrums, like a marching band was parading through my brain.

The cotton cover gradually slipped off my head. I wished it had stayed on.

I was hanging upside down.

Again.

Only this time, in shop class. My hands were tied behind my back. Beneath my head was a table saw.

Turned on.

The protective guard had—rather inconveniently—been removed. The saw's teeth blurred together into a continuous streak.

My Little Friend slowly slid out from beneath my T-shirt. It dangled in front of my face before the shoe-lace slipped completely off and fell onto the blade and—*zzzst!*

No more inhaler.

Looking over to my left, I saw Yardstick holding the end of a rope. The rest of the Tribe stood behind him, Sully included, watching me wriggle through the air.

Peashooter stepped up. "How's it hanging?"

If this is the best pun he can come up with, I should be the only one allowed to crack jokes.

"Oh, you know," I yelled, over the hum of the table saw. "Hanging by a thread."

Peashooter held up my backpack. "What've we got here?"

"That's mine!"

Rummaging inside, he pulled out my math textbook. "What's tonight's homework assignment?"

"Review pages thirty through thirty-two."

"Sucks that you have to carry this heavy textbook just for three measly pages." He flipped through. "Why not just bring home the ones you need and leave the rest of your book behind?"

He ran my math textbook across the table. The blade chewed through its pages, sending a fine dust of math equations flurrying straight into my face.

If I had any doubt that blade was real, it quickly faded.

"What other homework do you have?"

My language arts textbook was next.

Then world history.

One by one, Peashooter ran my textbooks through the saw until there were none left.

"Now what?" he grinned. "How about . . ."

He pulled out his staple remover. He pinched me by the nose and tugged.

"You?"

He let my nose go, sending my upturned body swinging back and forth through the air like a pendulum. There was about three feet between my neck and the blade.

"Yardstick!" Peashooter called out.

Yardstick shook his head. "I don't know about this. I don't think we should—"

"*Just do it!*"

Yardstick eased the rope downward as Peashooter recited: "*Down—certainly, relentlessly down! . . . How fearful . . . the proximity of the steel! . . . Death would have been a relief. . . .*"

I turned to Sully. "Can I get a hand here?"

"Sorry," she said. "My hands are tied."

Enough with the puns already!

"Remind me what this pop quiz is supposed to prove, exactly?"

"That even when death is imminent," Peashooter called out, "you're not afraid! A member of the Tribe never shows fear."

"Do I have to lose a limb to prove it to you—or can I just write an essay instead?"

Peashooter motioned to Yardstick to lower me even closer to the blade.

"Would you please stop doing that?!"

"Sorry," Yardstick said. "Boss's orders."

There couldn't have been but a couple inches between my face and the saw.

A drop of sweat rolled down to the tip of my nose. It hung there for a moment before finally dripping onto the table saw, bursting across the blade.

"All the way!" Peashooter suddenly ordered.

I took in a deep breath and pinched my eyes shut.

Start saying your prayers, Spence. Anything you want to get off your chest, now's the time. Better get cracking: Mom, I'm sorry I haven't been the best son and that I've made your life harder by being such a handful, and I know I've been acting really weird lately, but that's just because I've been angry at you and Dad because it's not fair that you two would make a decision like this without talking to me first, because this is my life too, and it's not fair that we had to move, because if we hadn't I wouldn't be suspended over a table saw right now, and I wish, I wish I had worn a fresh pair of underwear today, but now I'm going to die before I even get to kiss a girl, which totally sucks and—

The hum from the blade stopped.

I opened one eye. Then the other.

Everything seemed intact.

The Tribe had rolled the table saw out from under me at the very last moment. The crew was now crowded around me, snickering.

"Oh *hardy-har,*" I said. "Very funny."

Everybody busted out laughing.

"You should've seen the look on your face!" Peashooter guffawed.

"Can you cut me down now, *please?*"

Yardstick was about to release me when we all spotted Sporkboy leaning over the table saw. "These blades are pretty sharp, huh?"

He tapped his thumb on the blade's teeth.

I glanced over at Peashooter. That grin crept across his lips. "Think fast, Sporkboy!"

Peashooter flipped the switch on the table saw.

"Ben!" Compass reached out just in time to bat Sporkboy's hand away as the blade abruptly hummed back to life.

The pitch of the buzzing lifted up an octave for a split second.

Zzzm!

A fine red mist spritzed both Compass's and Sporkboy's face.

Compass's acne dribbled down his cheeks as if his zits were melting.

Wait—that's not acne. That's blood!

His eyes widened as he brought his hand up.

Where did the tip of his pinkie go?

"What were you thinking?!" Sully yelled at Peashooter.

"I was just trying to test Sporkboy's reflexes," he pleaded. "I didn't think . . ."

His words dwindled away.

Sully shot into action: "Yardstick, put Spencer down and grab as many paper towels as you can. Peashooter, get ice from the cafeteria. Sporkboy—*find his finger!*"

Sully grabbed Compass by his shoulders. "I need you to lie down."

He nodded and let her help him to the floor.

"This is going to hurt, but I got to apply pressure to slow the bleeding." She kept his arm elevated. She pulled out a rubber band from her pocket. Grabbing his pinkie and ring fingers, she wrapped the rubber band around the pinkie's lower knuckle.

"We've got to take him to a doctor," I said. I was glad to be back on my feet but I was still shaky—either from being upside down or from the sight of blood trickling down Compass's arm.

"Nobody leaves the building," Sully insisted. "Those are the rules."

"What are you going to do?" Compass whimpered to Sully.

She took a deep breath. "Cauterize it."

"You can't be serious!" I said, rocking back and forth.

"You got any better ideas?" Sully asked.

"Yeah! Take him to the emergency room!"

"No!" Compass quickly reanimated. "No emergency rooms, no doctors."

"But you just lost a finger!"

"Just the tip." He swallowed. "We made a pact. *Never leave the building.* . . ."

This was full-blown nuts.

"For a group that's supposed to not follow the rules," I said, "you sure have a lot of them!"

Compass's eyelids began to flutter. Wooziness was washing over him. He turned to Sully. "There's a Bunsen burner in the science lab. . . ."

"I'll need bandages from the nurse's office," Sully said. "And a metal ruler."

"What do you need a ruler for?" I asked.

"To heat up and press against the stump."

I felt my gag reflex spasm at the back of my throat.

"If we're really doing this, then let's go!" Sully ordered as she slung one of Compass's arms around her shoulder. Yardstick took the other.

"Found it! Found it!" Sporkboy suddenly shouted, holding the tip of Compass's pinkie in the air like it was the last bite of a french fry. "Three-second rule!"

BARBERSHOP IN THE BOILER ROOM

We buried ourselves in the boiler room later that night. Candles cast a grid of shadows through the pipes, and Griz the Grizzly was sprawled out on the floor like a rug. His helmet head was perched upright, so his blank eyes stared dumbly at me.

"It is time to honor one of our own." Peashooter placed his hands on Compass's shoulders. "You, Compass, have shown allegiance. You're a true hero."

Sporkboy started clapping wildly.

Yardstick added his applause.

Compass raised his hands in a gesture of light-headed gratitude, wincing as he waved with three quarters of his fingers. He presented his mummified pinkie to the rest of us and recited: *"At times he regarded the wounded soldiers in an envious way. He conceived persons with torn bodies to be peculiarly happy. He wished that he, too, had a wound . . ."*

Sporkboy and Yardstick cheered, reciting along with him: "... *a red badge of courage!*"

Compass believed in the Tribe so much that he was willing to lose a limb for them.

This was what would be expected from me when I joined.

If—*if*—I joined.

Once you're in—you're in for life.

Could I really do it?

Griz looked like he was pleading for my help. I knew how he felt.

"All right, everybody." Sully pulled out a milk crate and plopped it down on Griz's back, snapping me out of it. "Sully's Salon is open for business."

She held up a rusty pair of electric clippers and buzzed at the air.

"Listen up," Peashooter announced. "Tonight, in honor of Compass's great sacrifice, we all must follow in his footsteps and offer up something of ourselves."

Sporkboy blanched. "Are we cutting off our pinkies now?"

Peashooter was growing flustered. "In order to form a greater whole, the individual must surrender what he holds dear. Tonight—we shear ourselves of our individualism so we can become a stronger Tribe!"

"What's that supposed to mean?" Sporkboy asked.

Compass leaned over and whispered, "He wants us to shave our heads."

A sudden rush of protest passed through Yardstick. "But I like my hair. . . ."

Peashooter persisted. "Ever hear of esprit de corps?"

"I failed French," Sporkboy piped up.

"It's a military term. It means the morale of the unit. We cut our hair as a show of solidarity. Consider it an act of tribal camaraderie."

Yardstick averted his gaze. One of his dreadlocks slid into his face, the paper clip attached to the end swinging pendulously before his eyes.

"We're all doing this," Peashooter said. "No exceptions."

"What about her?" Compass nodded at Sully.

She didn't hesitate a second. "Any of you come near me and I'll cut off more than just your hair."

Nobody argued.

"Who's first?"

Peashooter sat down on the milk crate.

"I need a weed whacker." Sully wrapped a smock from art class around his neck and began to hack away at that dense crop of locks.

To be honest, the whole Tribe was a bit *unkempt* in the hair department. Each of their heads was topped by a wild thatch, which no shampoo had ventured into for a long time.

"I don't think this qualifies as hair anymore." Sully studied the clump she'd just severed from Peashooter's head.

"Funny," he said. "Just wait until it's your turn."

"Fat chance. *Next*."

"My turn, my turn!" Sporkboy squealed. "Just a little off the top, please."

"What's the rush, Sporky?" Compass snorted. "Squirrels living in your hair?"

"You're next, Compass," Peashooter said.

The sneer on Compass's lips dwindled. "I thought I already made my sacrifice."

"For the Tribe," Peashooter reminded.

"Some things we do in the name of science," Compass rationalized as he plopped onto the crate. "Others we do in the name of the Tribe."

Once Sully had mowed through the thicket on top of Compass's head, Sporkboy took his turn. Then Peashooter turned to Yardstick.

"Come on," Peashooter ordered. "We don't have all night."

Yardstick didn't move. He brought his arms up to his chest and bowed his chin.

"It'll grow back," Sully offered. "Promise."

Yardstick kept his eyes on the floor and slowly stepped forward. "What have I got left?"

"You've got us," Peashooter said. "That's all you need."

I was surprised to see how young Yardstick and the rest looked without all that hair hanging in their faces.

Amazing what a couple years between haircuts can do.

Even Peashooter. His translucent skin made him look like a newborn lab mouse.

"Last but not least." Peashooter nodded at me.

"No, thanks," I said. "I just got a trim. . . ."

"Nonnegotiable, sorry. But if it'll make you feel better, I'll bat my eyelashes and say *pwetty pwease*."

"My mom will kill me."

"You want to be one of us—or not?"

It was a good question. One I'd been asking myself more and more lately.

I looked to Yardstick. His face was washed of all emotion. Sporkboy, too.

I sat down on the crate.

"How'd you like that haircut to begin just below the neck?" I quoted from *The Outsiders*.

"Not bad." Peashooter looked impressed. "Now you're getting the hang of it."

I was. I had to keep up with the Tribe and all of their recitations somehow.

More and more, I was reading. Retaining.

Learning.

To the lemmings, textbooks did nothing but weigh our backpacks down.

But to the Tribe—they became bibles.

The Compass Book of Chemistry. The Yardstick Book of Algebra.

The Tribal Book of English Lit, King Peashooter Edition.

One thing Peashooter was right about: *Limited minds, limited havoc.*

Bigger minds most definitely mean bigger havoc.

Sully wrapped the smock around me. She leaned over and whispered, "I'll be gentle, I promise."

The buzz from the clippers sent a tremor through my neck.

Bzzt. I watched the first tuft of hair drift through the air like a feather, landing at my feet.

Bzzt. The next patch fell upon Griz's head. Then another.

Bzzt. Griz suddenly looked as if he was getting hair implants.

Compass took the opportunity to step up to the crate and elbow me in the ribs. "I need you to pick up some potassium nitrate for me."

"Potassium *what?*"

"*Saltpeter.* Peashooter wants me to whip up another batch of smoke bombs. I'm running low on a few ingredients. . . ."

"Hold still," Sully said as she continued to mow. "Don't want to lose an ear, do you?"

"Now that you mention it," Sporkboy said, leaning in on the other side of me, "think you could pick me up some bottle rockets?"

"What am I?" I asked. "A tribal delivery boy?"

"Think of it as going undercover," Peashooter insisted. "You're covertly slipping between two worlds without raising suspicion."

So, I'm not their inside man.

But an *outside* man.

"All done," Sully said. "Here. Take a look."

She handed me a cracked compact mirror. The fracture in

the glass ran directly down the middle, splitting the reflection of my freshly shorn head into halves.

Who was that supposed to be?

Me?

"Of all those in the army close to the commander none is more intimate than the secret agent," Peashooter recited. He slapped the palm of his hand on top of my new dome.

Whenever I was with Peashooter, I found myself getting swept up into his rhetoric, but the second I stepped away and attempted to reflect on what he had said, the fog of his words would dissipate from my brain.

"That's all fine and good for whoever said that," I responded. "But they probably weren't just glorified gofers."

"Are you challenging me?"

"I thought that's what you wanted from us," I said. "Stand up to the status quo."

Peashooter seemed ruffled. "I'm the *status quo* now?"

He started to pace. I hadn't gotten up from the milk crate yet.

"Not status quo," I started, noticing that Yardstick had moved up next to Sporkboy.

"Then what, exactly?"

"You mouth off about not being like all the other cliques in school," I said, slowly rising. "You say we should reject the petty tyranny of the in-crowd, but you guys have become the inner-most in-crowd. You're like the *inner* in-crowd!"

I was surrounded by a ring of shiny scalps.

Peashooter was right in my face. He didn't flinch, so I tried not to flinch either.

I lifted my chin. Peashooter lifted his.

"Don't forget who found *you*," he muttered under his breath. "I saved you from the status quo."

"You're like everybody else here at Greenfield. More than you know."

Peashooter's fingers slowly curled into a fist.

"Barbershop's closed, boys," Sully said, breaking us up. "Bonfire time."

". . . Fire?" I asked.

"Come see for yourself."

• • •

Sully led me up to the roof, where we built a shaggy bonfire. She lit a match and tossed it into the heap of recently cut hair. Loose curls burst into flame, and the smell of burned hair filled my nose.

"You're like a den mother to the others, aren't you?"

"Yeah, right." She half laughed. "I'm a real regular Wendy Darling."

"Who?"

"From *Peter Pan*."

Note to self: Read more books.

"Peashooter always says knowledge is power."

"Just not more power than he has," I suggested. "Must get kind of lonely being the only girl among the boys."

"*One girl is worth more use than twenty boys*," Sully said.

Another book reference. It was hard to keep up with them all.

There was a hiss and crackle from the fire engulfing the bits of clippings. The flare cast a long shadow across Sully's face, half hidden behind her hair.

"How come you don't cut your hair?" I asked.

"It's how I mark the time away from home."

It was well past her lower back.

I brought my hand up and tucked her hair behind her ear, exposing her cheeks. I could see freckles on her pale face.

"It's hard to see you underneath there," I said. "It's like you're hiding."

As quickly as I caught sight of her, Sully dipped her chin. Hair and shadow swallowed her face. "Who says I'm hiding?"

"Sorry . . ."

"Just 'cause I'm a girl doesn't mean you can get googly-eyed on me, okay?" she said. "I don't need to deal with some puppy-dog crush."

"Who says I've got a crush?"

"Sure act like it."

"Well, sure sounds like *somebody's* got a high opinion of herself."

"I'm not some sugar-and-spice-and-everything-nice kind of

girl, okay? If you want somebody to bat their eyelashes at you, stick to the chicks at school."

"You *are* a chick at school. You're more at school than any other chick I know!"

"You know what I mean."

Silence.

Sully ran her hand over the slope of my scalp. "You don't look all that bad with a shaved head."

The two of us stared at the embers by our feet. They looked like the coiled wires inside a lightbulb being turned off, low-wattage orange diminishing into ash.

"Why haven't you asked me for anything from outside?" I blurted. "Everybody else has."

She thought about it for a moment. "There is one thing. . . ."

"Name it."

"I was wondering if maybe you could . . ."

"What?"

"I was wondering if you could visit my . . ."

Her voice trailed off.

"Visit who? Your family?"

"Never mind," she said. "We should go back inside."

• • •

Walking home, I could see the sun seeping through the trees. The sky was slowly growing pink. Morning was almost here.

Sure wish Sully was here to see this with me.

I walked past one of her MISSING flyers stapled to a telephone pole.

I was exhausted. All I wanted was to slip into bed before starting the day over again, even for just five minutes.

Just for my own mental mathematics, I tried calculating how much time I was actually spending at Greenfield, squandering the first part of my day trudging through classes, then detention, then slipping back at night when no one was around.

If my calculations were correct, there were three hours that I was actually at home, eating dinner with Mom before turning in early, just to crawl out through my bedroom window.

If you told me that I'd be going out of my way to hang out at school twenty-one hours out of each day, I would've said you must be mistaking me for some kind of academic maggot.

I had wedged open the window of my bedroom with a butter knife when I'd left earlier that evening, making sure it didn't seal shut behind me. That way, when I got home, all I had to do was jimmy the window and crawl back in.

"Look who decided to finally come home."

I froze, straddling the windowsill. The voice came from a corner of my bedroom, still hidden by early morning shadows.

". . . Mom?"

The light flickered on, revealing Mom in her bathrobe, sitting at my desk. From the bags under her eyes, it was easy to see that she wasn't rested.

I crawled the rest of the way inside and fell onto my bed, staring up at the ceiling.

No sleep for me.

"What are you doing still up?"

"Waiting for my son to come back from wherever he was all night."

"I just went out for a walk."

"Five hours ago?"

"You've been waiting for me?"

"Where did your hair go?"

"You don't like it?"

"Why would you cut it all off? You've always had such beautiful hair. . . ."

"It's just hair, Mom."

"I don't even recognize you anymore."

"It'll grow back."

"I wasn't talking about your hair!" Mom stopped, closed her eyes, and took a breath. She exhaled—slowly. "Start explaining."

"Can you just let me sleep for a little bit?"

"Try again."

"It's not what you think. Honest."

"Please—tell me what I'm thinking. And while you're at it, give me one good reason why I shouldn't padlock you inside this room for the rest of your life!"

"It's a fire hazard?"

"Spencer." Mom's voice strained. It sounded like her esophagus had collapsed.

The first tear to roll down her cheek caught me by surprise. I didn't expect that.

The second and third only made matters worse.

"Mom?"

She didn't say anything at first, just rubbed her hand over each cheek. "I thought we could do this. You and me. I thought we could make it work."

"I'm sorry," I said.

"I can't do this alone."

We both were sniffling now, Mom and me, watching the morning sun seep through the bedroom window. Then my alarm started to ring.

Time to go to school.

GHOST STORY NUMBER FOUR: SULLY

Chosen Name: <u>Sully</u>
Given Name: <u>Sully Tulliver</u>
Area of Study: <u>Biology</u>
Weapon of Choice: <u>Slingshot</u>
Last seen: <u>7th grade</u>
Notes: <u>Green eyes. Auburn hair. Freckles along the bridge</u> <u>of her nose. Sharpshooter. Heard her laugh once. Doesn't</u> <u>like talking about herself much. Marches to the beat</u> <u>of her own tribal drum.</u>

SULLY FIELD NOTES ENTRY #1:
LOCATION: ROOFTOP
TIME: 12:00 MIDNIGHT

SULLY: I've always been a bit of an etymologist. . . . "Circle, circle. Dot, dot. Now you've got a cootie shot."

Sully loved bugs as a kid. Back in elementary school, she carried a magnifying glass wherever she went. She would set up shop on the playground and inspect kids for nits, all through recess.
Guess who she had a crush on?

None other than Riley Callahan himself.

SULLY: Even back then, he had the most immaculate hair you'd ever laid eyes on.

When Riley asked Sully for his own personal examination in first grade, she nearly peed in her pants.

SULLY: I sat him down on the swing set and held my magnifying glass about an inch away from his hairline. It was hard to keep my wrist from shaking.

Only problem was—Sully examined him for so long that she ended up magnifying the heat of the sun through the lens.

It was like aiming a laser directly onto Riley's scalp.

Riley smelled something burning, but he had no idea it was his own hair. Sully realized what was happening when all that fancy styling mousse caught fire. Riley's head went up in a blaze. He started screaming, swatting at his head. All the other kids watched him run 'round and 'round the playground until their teacher finally put out the flames with her coat.

Riley said Sully set his hair on fire on purpose.

Her private practice shut itself down shortly thereafter.

SULLY FIELD NOTES ENTRY #2:
LOCATION: LIBRARY
TIME: 1:00 P.M.

I only had to flip through a few yearbooks before I found her photo. The picture was the same one her parents had used for her MISSING flyer.
Someone had written alongside her face:
<u>COOTIE CATCHER</u>

SULLY: Riley got everybody to call me that. "Circle, circle. Square, square. Now you've got it everywhere."

Whenever Sully walked through the halls, she would hear from behind her back, "Watch out! The Cootie Catcher's coming through!"
She was never able to outrun the nickname.

SULLY: It got to the point where I couldn't take it anymore.
ME: So that's why you joined the Tribe? Because of a nickname?
SULLY: You'd understand if you'd been called something like that your whole life.

ME: There has to be a bigger reason than that. . . . Why did you leave?

SULLY: I don't want to talk about it.

ME: Okay. Sorry.

SULLY: Riley better wear a shower cap to school tomorrow.

ME: You gonna futz with the sprinkler system or something?

SULLY: Pediculus humanus capitis.

ME: What's that?

SULLY: You'll see . . . "Circle, circle. Knife, knife. Now you've got it all your life."

REVENGE
OF THE
COOTIE CATCHER

The baseball cap worked for thirty seconds.

I slipped through Greenfield's front doors with the brim pulled down as far as it would go. Ten paces into the building and Pritchard snatched it off.

"No caps in school," he droned. Then he realized who he was addressing. "*Spencer?* What happened to your hair?"

"Trying to be more efficient, sir. Now that I don't have to wash my hair in the morning, I have an extra thirty-three-point-six seconds to focus on writing my personal memoir."

Pritchard wasn't amused.

"Pick your hat up from my office at the end of school."

• • •

Things didn't get itchy until third period.

Fifteen minutes from the end of class, Mr. Rorshuck dropped a bomb on us.

"Pop quiz," he announced as he handed them out. "You have fifteen minutes."

Sitting directly behind Sarah Haversand, I noticed her scratching the top of her head as if deep in thought.

"Start . . . *now!*"

I attacked the first question.

I spotted Martin Mendleson absentmindedly digging the tip of his pencil into his scalp.

By the time I finished question #2, something fell onto my paper.

Leaning over, I watched it crawl across an equation.

A wriggling digit.

"Mr. Rorshuck?" I raised my hand, hoping to control the mounting panic in my voice.

"Not in the middle of a quiz, Mr. Pendleton. You know the rules."

"But this is—uh, I think this is an emergency."

Sarah kept scraping her scalp, harder now. A squirming snow flurry scattered across her quiz sheet. She leapt to her feet, screaming, pointing toward her desk.

"What *is* that?!"

Everybody turned toward her, suddenly scratching at their own heads.

"Eyes on your own paper, everyone," Rorshuck called out.

I could see the lightbulb go off in Sarah's brain.

"Lice?" she yelled. *"Lice!"*

Immediately, the rest of the class went cross-eyed, looking up toward their own hairlines.

"Li-li-liiiiiice!" Sarah's scream erupted from her throat like molten lava pouring forth from a volcano.

Kids soared out of their seats. "LICE! LICE! LICE!"

Rorshuck yelled after them. "The quiz isn't over yet!"

But it was too late. The bell rang and the outbreak began.

I looked up to see a loosened fiberglass panel. Through the gap, I spotted the disembodied grin of none other than the Cootie Catcher herself.

• • •

"We have a nit-free policy here," Assistant Principal Pritchard said over the intercom later that day. "Until we're positive that students no longer have any egg sacs in their hair, they will not be allowed back in school."

The next day, there were so many buzz cuts in the hallway, I lost count.

It almost felt like I had started a trend.

When I first saw Riley Callahan's freshly shorn head, I couldn't help but feel a sudden swell of pride.

Riley glanced over and made eye contact with me. There was

a haunted look in his eyes. Almost hollow. There was barely any resemblance between the Riley standing before me now and that clear-complexioned, perfectly coiffed kid I'd bumped into when I got here.

I could hardly recognize him anymore.

• • •

I snuck up to the roof during lunch with my food. It was just about the only spot left where I could think.

Pendleton. Table for one, please.

I looked at the back of my milk carton and—*surprise, surprise*—found Sporkboy staring right back at me, smiling from his MISSING picture.

It was Benjamin's yearbook photo: Same carroty hair. Same chubby cheeks. Same smile.

After I finished my milk, I tore off the back section of the carton, slipping Sporkboy's picture into my pocket, like a baseball card.

Here's a Benjamin Greenwood original. Mint condition. Not even a single crease in the cardboard. Collect them all.

I wondered if my photograph would pop up on a carton of two-percent one day. Make your way onto the back of your own milk, and you're a team member for life.

Who are we? We are the *Milk Carton Kids.*

Have you seen us?

"Is this roof taken?" someone asked from behind me.

Sully.

"Why, no. . . . Have a seat."

We split my meal between us.

Impromptu picnic.

"It's hard to spot you in the hallways," she said. "Too many bald heads."

"That reminds me." I pulled out a square sheet of paper from my backpack. "I have something for you."

"What's this?"

I folded the sheet in half. Then folded it again.

Then I folded each corner into the center.

I flipped it over and folded all four corners toward the center on the other side.

I stuck my thumbs and forefingers into the flap pockets, bringing all four fingers together in the center so that they made a sharp point.

"Ta-da," I said. "Your own personal cootie catcher."

I slipped behind Sully and began to pick at her hair.

"Look at me," I said. "I'm an orangutan searching for nits!"

"Quit it."

"*Mm-mm!* It's a regular monkey buffet up here!"

"That's not funny!" She laughed.

"All you can eat!"

We both stopped laughing and neither of us said anything for the longest time.

"You're giving me those googly eyes again," she said finally. "What are you thinking?"

"Do you miss home?"

"Sometimes."

"Don't you ever wish you could go back?"

"I guess I could if I really wanted to." She shrugged her shoulders. "But why would I, when I've got everything I need right here?"

"You guys should've taken over a shopping mall instead," I said. "At least then we could go to the movies or something."

"Did you just ask me out on a date?"

"No!"

"Good—because I'm way older than you."

"You're not *that* much older than me."

"Two years, at least!"

"I've been told I'm very mature for my age."

Sully laughed. I liked it when I could make her laugh.

"Just think," she said. "Before long, you'll be one of us."

One of us.

For Sully, I would shed the rest of my life like a butterfly crawling out of its cocoon.

This would be my new start. My clean slate.

Just like Mom wanted.

GHOST STORY NUMBER FIVE: COMPASS

Chosen Name: <u>Compass</u>
Given Name: <u>Jimmy Winters</u>
Area of Study: <u>Chemistry</u>
Weapon of Choice: <u>Compass-chucker, X-ACTO knuckles</u>
Last seen: <u>8th grade</u>
Notes: <u>Second in command. Major superiority complex.</u>
<u>More insecurities than most. Highly volatile.</u>

COMPASS FIELD NOTES ENTRY #1:
LOCATION: LIBRARY
TIME: 10:00 P.M.

It wasn't too difficult to find Jimmy Winters's photograph in the yearbook. Someone had already played connect-the-dots with his pimples.

COMPASS: Acne vulgaris has run in my family for generations.

Compass always has a crop of creamy mushroom-capped acne sprouting from the surface of his oily skin.

Even today, the outbreak of whiteheads stretches over his nose, his forehead, his cheeks—like a cluster of toadstools about to pop.

COMPASS: I tried benzoyl peroxide, prescription medication, even alpha-hydroxy acid baths. But the pimples grow back.

His classmates always made fun of him.
"Look at the size of that oil slick!"
"Don't walk behind him. You might slip."
"Bet you could funnel that oil from your face and fuel my dad's car!"

COMPASS: You get used to it. After a while, you just grow thick skin.

Thick, scaly, red skin. With whiteheads.

COMPASS FIELD NOTES ENTRY #2:
LOCATION: SOCCER FIELD
TIME: 12:00 MIDNIGHT

Compass asked me to run an errand for him before Thanksgiving.

He wanted me to sneak onto the soccer field with a flashlight and a pair of rubber gloves to hunt for . . .

COMPASS: Amanita muscaria.
ME: Musca-what?
COMPASS: Mushrooms. From the fly agaric genus? They're a highly psychoactive basidiomycete fungus. Pretty poisonous stuff. They sprout along the soccer fields at night. We have to pick them before Mr. Simms mows in the morning.
ME: What do you want with a bunch of mushrooms?
COMPASS: Just a little science experiment.

I had to get down on my hands and knees to sift through the grass.

Then I had to pluck each mushroom from the soil and hold it up to the flashlight, just to see if it fit Compass's criteria:

White-gilled. Deep red cap. White spots.

A. muscaria!

The resemblance between the toadstool and Compass's complexion was uncanny, but I figured I shouldn't mention it.

Sore subject.

COMPASS FIELD NOTES ENTRY #3:
LOCATION: SCIENCE LAB
TIME: 1:00 A.M.

Before he became Compass, Jimmy had been at the top of his class. A's in every subject. Particularly the sciences.

Chemistry was his jam.

There was one event every year that Jimmy counted down the days to: the Greenfield Middle School Annual Science Fair.

Jimmy had won first place two years in a row. He wouldn't settle for second on his eighth-grade presentation. There was one more blue ribbon in his future, and he'd stop at nothing until it was pinned to his lapel.

COMPASS: For my project that year, I had been thinking about isolating certain strains of food-borne bacteria. But my chemistry teacher, Mr. Fitzpatrick, said, "No pathogenic agents." I had to keep it safe.

Jimmy settled for something simple:
<u>Developing his own supermushroom.</u>
The day before the science fair, Mr. Fitzpatrick

had Jimmy stand before his science class to explain his project. Jimmy was never one for public presentations, mainly for complexion-related reasons.

COMPASS: I told the class I would be winning the blue ribbon with an inorganic compound I'd developed that would increase crop yields by forty percent. To illustrate the success of my macronutrients, I'd decided to use my fertilizer to grow a giant fiber head mushroom. . . .

But someone at the back of the classroom had apparently snorted. "<u>Fiber head</u>?" they said. "You mean, like, a <u>whitehead</u>? 'Cause I can count a couple fiber heads about to burst across your nose right now!"

COMPASS: I'd show them. I'd win first place and head to nationals and win there, too. Then I'd come back to Greenfield and every last student would beg for my forgiveness.

He'd begun his Nobel acceptance speech already. Jimmy's science project was a piece of cake. He would grow his own mushroom, from spore to sprout, in a matter of minutes.

COMPASS: Amateur stuff, really. All it took was one shoe box full of soil, a household microwave, some fungal-tissue cultures—and my own special blend of growth hormones.

Jimmy had already calculated the proper amount of moisture and fertilizer he'd need for germination.

COMPASS: But not too much. A little dab will do you. . . .

Jimmy would microwave the mycelium right there in the cafeteria, getting that mushroom to grow before the judges' very eyes.

COMPASS: See you in the winner's circle. . . .

The not-so-simple part? Keeping the other students from tampering with it.
Somebody had poured red food coloring into his spore samples the night before.
<u>Science fair sabotage.</u>

COMPASS: When it was my turn to present my project, I flipped the switch—and sure enough, the machine warmed my spores. In seconds, I could see tiny fiber heads budding up from their shoe-box bed. They kept growing. Thirty times their normal diameter in three seconds!

Stopping the mushrooms from growing wasn't something Jimmy had factored into his experiment. They inflated outward, their red caps overflowing.

None of the judges knew what to do. The spores looked like water balloons about to burst. Was this a part of the experiment?

The judges took a step back, two steps, three—until:

BOOM!

A fine mist of red-splotched spores exploded out from his crop, covering the judges, Jimmy, and every student within a ten-yard radius.

Instant pimples.

One of Jimmy's competitors started laughing, pointing at our crushed junior scientist and his spore-spewing project.

More laughter. Before long, the whole cafeteria was guffawing at Jimmy's science project.

The blood in his body rushed into his head. His face went purple.

And just like a whitehead pinched between your fingertips, he popped.

COMPASS: "Think you can all laugh at me?" I yelled. "I'll show you! All of you! We'll see who laughs last!"

After the science fair, nobody ever saw him again. But Jimmy's been here all this time, just beneath Greenfield's skin, waiting to rise up once more.

POP QUIZ: THINGS TO BE THANKFUL FOR THIS THANKSGIVING

We had a full four-day weekend ahead of us. From Thursday through Sunday, the hallways at Greenfield Middle would be empty.

No students, no teachers. Not even Mr. Simms would be hanging around.

The whole school would be utterly abandoned.

Doors locked, lights off. Completely vacated.

Well. *Almost.*

• • •

I had made up my mind.

I'd tell the Tribe I wasn't joining their ranks. No matter the consequences, I wouldn't be revoking my Still Student Status.

What was the best way to break it to them? Let's explore my options:

Option A: *It's not you, it's me. . . .*

Option B: *Been nice knowing you fellas, but I just found out I'm being transferred to a swanky private school in Vermont. Catch y'all at the class reunion.*

Option C: *Things have gone too far. I'm in way over my head. When I first found out about the Tribe, it felt like I'd met a group of like-minded, marginalized kids who wanted me for me. But the more time passes, the more I realize I'm changing, and if this is who I have to be in order to join, then I won't do it. Not to my mom. I'm out.*

I wanted to tell Sully first. Maybe she'd even decide to come back with me. . . .

One more time and that's it, I swore to myself. *You can sneak out just one last time.*

But first—I had to get through dinner.

You've never seen a man tuck into a turkey as fast as me.

"You don't have to eat the whole thing by yourself, you know," Mom said. "There are two of us here."

This was our first holiday dinner on our own, and we hadn't talked for most of the meal.

"Almost forgot." Mom rushed back to the kitchen.

She returned to the table holding her hand behind her back. "I saved something special for you. I know how much you love them."

She brought her hand up to me, trying to smile.

A turkey wishbone.

I stared at the forked breastbone pinched between her fingers, the tiniest fleck of meat still clinging to it.

Dad and I always tug-of-warred with the wishbone.

Mom knew that.

"Spencer?"

I took hold of one end and started pulling. "Wonder how Dad's doing."

"Beats me." Mom pulled back on her end of the bone. "Why don't you call him up? He owes you one."

"Dad doesn't owe me anything." I yanked hard, snapping the wishbone in half.

Mom flinched. She had the larger bit of bone.

"Make a wish, Mom."

• • •

Thanksgiving is a time to show appreciation for all the wonderful things that have happened throughout the year.

Walking back to Greenfield, I took the time to reflect upon what I had to be thankful for.

Let's see . . . I'm thankful the tryptophan from the turkey kicked in, sending Mom to bed a little earlier than usual tonight.

I'm thankful for whoever leaves the window open in the industrial arts class.

I'm thankful for having packed a flashlight.

But I'm most thankful for My Little Friend. After having him destroyed in the shop, it was good to have him back by my side. More like my chest, actually. We've been through thick and thinly oxygenated blood cells together.

I took a puff before crawling through the window.

Finding Sully without alerting the others would be a challenge. I couldn't just call out her name. That would draw too much attention.

Passing through the left bat wing of the building, I noticed a glow emanating from behind the science lab's door. A cerulean light flickered across the floor.

I placed my hand on the knob.

Unlocked.

Opening the door, I discovered the blue tongue of a Bunsen burner lapping at the darkness.

Sully stood before the continuous stream of flammable gas as if it were a tiny campfire, casting her shadow across the classroom walls.

"Sully," I said, catching my breath. "Just who I was looking for . . ."

"You found me." She managed to smile, but she remained right where she was.

I took another step inside the lab.

"There's something I need to tell you."

Peashooter popped out from under a desk.

"You've passed your final pop quiz," he said. "Congrats— you're almost one of us."

Almost?

I heard the door shut behind me, jolting me forward. I turned around and found Yardstick, Sporkboy, and Compass standing behind Peashooter.

Graffitied across the length of Sporkboy's arm was: *MY KID IS AN HONOR ROLL STUDENT.*

The three boys raised their javelins over their heads and sounded the battle cry.

Peashooter signaled for silence.

"On nights like these," he proclaimed to his Tribe, "we point our noses at the stars and howl long and wolf-like."

Sporkboy tilted his head back and howled. Compass and Yardstick added to the chorus.

"It's our ancestors," Peashooter continued, "dead and dust, howling through the centuries and through us!"

Sporkboy lead the Tribe through another round of howls. Peashooter and Sully joined in, making it sound like a wolf pack had been let loose in the building.

Compass pulled out a coat hanger that had been unraveled and straightened, with one end bent into a shape I couldn't make out. He held the twisted knot over the Bunsen burner's flame.

"Break out the marshmallows," I said. "Love me some s'mores."

"Sorry—no s'mores for you." Peashooter shook his head. His complexion looked cobalt-colored from the Bunsen burner's glow.

"Then . . . what's the hanger for?"

He rolled up the sleeve on his left arm, exposing the bulb of his shoulder.

There, rising up from the rest of his flesh, was a spiral of pink skin.

Scar tissue.

"A scar nobly got, or a noble scar, is a good livery of honor," Peashooter recited. "Shakespeare said that."

"Then poke Shakespeare with that thing—not me!"

"We all have one," Compass said. "Look."

The rest of the Tribe bared their shoulders. Under the blue light I could make out the patterns in their cauterized skin.

It was a version of the Tribe's stick figure, spear raised over its head.

I turned to Sully.

"You too?"

Sully pulled up her sleeve—and sure enough, there it was, hugging her shoulder.

"No thanks." I took a step back. "My body's not an option for tribal product placement."

"Hold him down." Peashooter motioned to Yardstick.

Before I could even make a break for it, Yardstick had me bent over the desk.

"Sorry," he whispered.

Sporkboy grabbed my hands and pinned me in place. He leaned over and said, "Pretty cool, huh? Just wait till you see it on yourself."

"Joke's over, guys. Let me go, okay?"

"The thing with sterilization, see," Compass started, "is that you want to maximize the temperature and minimize the luminosity."

"Now's *really* not the time for a science lesson. . . ."

Sporkboy yanked back the sleeve of my shirt and uncovered my skin.

"By opening up the air hole as far as it will go"—Compass kept going—"you get this perfectly blue blaze. The hottest component to the flame you don't even see. The invisible tip of the inner flame is where things get *really* hot."

"Let me go!"

"Too late to back out now." Peashooter shook his head. "You're one of us, Spencer. And when you join the Tribe, you carry the mark."

"I don't want to be one of you!"

"That's your fear speaking. Trust us, Spencer—you never have to be afraid again. Not with us on your side."

My eyes widened as Compass brought the coat hanger directly before my face. The tip of the hanger had turned into an orange knot of hot wire.

"Quit wiggling," Sporkboy muttered. "You'll ruin it."

"Time out time out time out time out . . ."

No matter how much I struggled, they wouldn't let me go.

"The pain is temporary," Peashooter said. "But the pride is forever."

Somebody took my hand.

Looking up, I saw it was Sully.

"Bite down on this." She slipped a pencil past my lips. "It's okay to close your eyes. I did."

I squeezed my eyes shut as Compass pressed the end of the coat hanger against my shoulder.

"This is gonna sting." I don't recall who said that.

Quick, Spence: go to a safe place in your mind.

Your own deserted island.

The Alaskan tundra.

With Dad.

I bit down.

The pencil snapped. Through the splinters on my tongue, I tasted the salty tang of graphite.

Between my gritted teeth, a roar erupted and echoed through the empty halls of Greenfield.

"Done," Peashooter said. "You can let him go."

Yardstick and Sporkboy released me.

Only Sully kept holding my hand.

I glanced down at my shoulder. Reddened flesh, bits of coconut skin flaking off around the seared edges of my new wound.

I'd been branded.

Part III: December

First take the plank out of your own eye, and then you will see clearly to remove the speck from your brother's eye.
—Matthew 7:5

MILK CARTON KIDS

ow late was it? My eyes wandered over to the alarm clock. 3:42 a.m.

I flipped onto my back.

Someone was staring at me.

Several someones. I could see cheeks, white as paper. Eyes, ringed in black, blending in with the shadows.

They were standing perfectly still. Not saying a word.

Smiling.

Ladies and gentlemen . . . the Tribe has left the building.

I reached over and switched on my bedside lamp. Light burned through every shadow.

It was just their MISSING flyers.

The rest of Greenfield knew them as Jack Cumberland. Benjamin Greenwood. Jimmy Winters. But to me they were Yardstick, Sporkboy, and Compass.

Sully was still Sully.

Almost had the whole set.

• • •

3:43 a.m.

Time had slowed to sludge. There's no way I was falling asleep.

The burn was beginning to heal.

Slowly.

The singed skin had scabbed over, as if the tribesman on my shoulder was wearing a scaly suit of red protective armor.

Is this what I signed up for?

The only clique that should get branded like this is a herd of cattle.

So much for not following the herd.

I had a week.

One week left as a student. One week of being a boy who suffers through homework and steps in poop quizzes. One more week before leaving everything behind for good.

"Nobody can know you're leaving," Peashooter had said. "Not your parents, not your friends. *Nobody.*"

I was becoming one of them—whether I wanted to or not.

There was no turning back now.

I turned off the light and everything slipped back into darkness.

What was I expecting?

My eyes adjusted to the dark—and I found their smiling faces on the flyers again. Now they looked like ghosts. Nothing but sheets of paper possessed by the dead.

Sweet dreams, Spence . . . .

SNOW DAY (OF THE DEAD)

When I woke up, the world outside my window had gone all white.

"Ten inches and counting," the weatherman said. "Bet there's gonna be a bunch of happy campers when we start calling out school closings."

Come on, Mr. Anchorman—say the magic words: *Snow day*.

He began listing off closings alphabetically: "Albemarle Middle, Anderson High, Bellevue Academy will only have a half day. . . ."

It took him forever to reach the G's.

Come on, just say it: *Greenfield Middle*.

One more time: *Greenfield Middle*.

A little bit louder now: *Greenfield Middle*!

"Congratulations," Mom said. "Guess who's not going to school today?"

If she only knew.

● ● ●

I huffed the two miles between my house and Greenfield. The streets had been wiped away in white. Parked cars were nothing more than lumps. The world had been bleached.

I found the building half buried. No footprints stretched over the sidewalks. Not a single tire tread wound through the parking lot.

There, sitting in the window of one of the classrooms, was Sully, gazing at the outside world.

"What are you doing here?" I could barely hear her through the glass.

"Snow day! Thought you might wanna go play."

"We're not supposed to leave the building. . . ."

"Come on," I said. "Just to the soccer fields."

"Somebody might see us."

"Ten minutes."

"I can't."

"Why? Because your boyfriend says you're not allowed to?"

"Jealous?"

"*Hardly.*"

Sully turned her head to make sure nobody was behind her. "Five minutes."

"Not a minute more." I held up a gloved hand. "Scout's honor."

We raided the lost-and-found and pulled out a boy's jacket for Sully. It was a few sizes too big, but it would do. She snitched a pair of mismatched mittens.

"Ever wonder whose stuff this used to be?" she asked.

"Long gone now—whoever they were."

"Kinda sad, when you think about it," she said. "They're like ghosts."

Maybe Sully was beginning to think she belonged inside the lost-and-found box too.

"I'm sure they won't mind you wearing them for a while," I said, forcing a smile.

"Hope not."

We had a smooth white stretch of untouched snow totally to ourselves. Sully dropped onto her back, arms outstretched. She fanned her hands up and down, plowing through the snow until a set of cotton-white wings sprouted out from her sides.

"I haven't made a snow angel since I was, like, six or something."

"It shows," I said. "Your snow angel sucks."

"Shut up."

"I'm sorry—but it's true."

"Your face sucks."

"At least I know how to make a snow angel."

"Oh yeah?"

"*Yeah.*"

"Prove it."

There we were, suddenly in the thick of a snow angel duel. With one angel done, we'd stand up, take two steps over to one side, and start all over again.

Before long, nearly the whole field was covered.

"Looks heavenly," Sully joked.

But you know what? Being with Sully felt pretty heavenly to me.

Too cheesy? *Fair enough.*

Then we had a snowball fight.

There had to have been thirty feet between my face and her fist—but one fastball later, my nose was nearly crushed under the weight of her first pitch.

"No fair," I yelled. "Warn me next time. . . ."

"Wouldn't be much of a fight if I told you my every move, now, would it?"

Sully quick-fired another.

"Ow!"

"Got you on the run now!"

Barreling through a barrage of snowballs, I tackled her, sending us both buckling over backward. We landed with a muffled thud on top of one of her snow angels.

"Angel down!" I yelled.

Sully laughed and her breath fogged up before her face. It was as if a ghost were launching out from her lungs.

Things suddenly got quiet between us, and I imagined Sully, years from now—still the smartest girl I would ever meet, hovering above students four or five years younger than her.

Then ten years.

Twenty.

"How's your shoulder?" she asked, breaking the silence.

"Getting better, I guess."

"Does it hurt?"

"Does it matter?"

Sully dipped her chin. "I should be going back inside now."

"Your lips look chapped."

"They are."

"Here," I said, fumbling through my back pocket. "Have some ChapStick."

"You shouldn't share your ChapStick with other people."

"Why?"

"You never know what germs they might have."

"That's okay," I said. "I don't care if I catch your germs."

"How romantic."

She said romantic. You heard her say it, right?

"You can keep the ChapStick," I said.

"Really?"

"All yours." I nodded.

"Thank you."

I watched her roll the ChapStick over her lips.

"Strawberry," she said. "My favorite."

"Mine too."

"You sure you don't want any? Your lips look like they could use some. . . ."

"That's okay." I shook my head. "Don't wanna get your germs or anything. . . ."

Sully's face was only a few inches away from mine. Our breath fogged up between us—and for that one moment, just for a split second, it felt like the whole soccer field had melted into a mist of our exhales. She started to lean forward. . . .

The sound of glass being shattered stopped her.

Sully quickly lifted her head and looked toward the building. The window to Rorshuck's classroom was broken.

No sign of who did it.

"I've got to go," she said, standing up and running back.

"What's wrong?"

"Nothing," she called over her shoulder. "I'll see you tomorrow."

LIVING TARGET PRACTICE

There was a note waiting for me in my locker the next day. My presence had been requested by Peashooter.

Slipping into the last stall, I locked myself inside before climbing up on the toilet.

I popped open the fiberglass panel and ducked my head in.

"Took you long enough," Peashooter said, waiting for me on the other side.

"I'll bring roses next time."

He'd graffitied himself again. On his left arm he'd written: *ROBIN HOODLUM.*

On his right, from wrist to elbow, it read: *MERRY MADMEN.*

"Step into my office," he said, pulling me up.

We crawled above Mr. Rorshuck's class.

Easing back the panel by a couple inches, we had a perfect vantage point of all the students sitting below. They lazily gazed at Rorshuck as he attacked the blackboard with his chalk.

Peashooter stared down at the class, lost in thought.

"I had a dream last night," he said. "It came to me as a question: Why stick with just one school?"

"What? You looking to transfer or something?"

"Do you know how many schools there are in this district alone? This county? *This state?* Imagine how many kids there are out there just like us, looking for a group that they can call their own."

I could sense where Peashooter was going with all this.

"Now ask yourself: How many tribes do you think we could create? Why stick with just one school when we can grow? Branch out? Increase our numbers?"

"You mean franchise tribes?"

"I mean *revolution*. And it all begins with a few transfer students moving to a new school. Taking it over from the inside. . . . Beautiful, isn't it?"

Peashooter had totally gone full-blown Napoleon.

"A kid can dream, can't he?" He flashed his devilish grin at me, as if to say he was only joking. I only half believed him. "Let's practice."

He handed me one of his hollowed-out ballpoint pens and placed a sheet of paper between us. When there was enough noise below, he tore off a corner of the paper and slipped it into his mouth. A moment later, he stuck his tongue out, displaying a perfectly balled-up wad.

"Now you."

I had a hard time summoning up any spit. "My mouth feels like a desert."

"Nervous?"

I gave myself a half dozen paper cuts on my tongue before finally wetting the spitball down. "Locked and loaded," I said.

"Aim higher than the actual point you want to hit," he said. "Watch and learn."

He brought the pen up to his mouth. He inhaled through his nose, funneling air into his nasal cavity, down his throat, and directly into the open end of his dart gun—*Pfft!*

That spit wad shot out from the barrel of Peashooter's pen and landed smack-dab in Sarah Haversand's perfectly coiffed hair—*Splat!*

Sarah swatted the back of her head, unaware of the pellet that had just adhered itself to her blond locks. *Bull's-eye!*

"That's how it's done," Peashooter said. "Your turn."

"I want Rorshuck."

"Check out the cojones on you," he said. "I'm impressed."

"Here goes nothing. . . ."

Deep breath.

Ready.

Aim.

Fire!

My first spit wad splatted against the equation Mr. Rorshuck had just scribbled on the blackboard. He spun around, staring down his class.

"Who did that?"

The class stared blankly back at him, as stunned as their teacher.

"Who was it?"

Time was running out. If I was going to make my target, I had to do it now.

"Answer me!"

I went ahead and answered. I answered him loud and clear. I answered by leaning over the open fiberglass and firing up another spitball, hitting Mr. Rorshuck directly in the forehead. The spit wad struck his skin with such force that it left a splatter-pattern of saliva and pulped-up paper across his receding hairline. *Perfect hit!*

I turned to Peashooter, victorious. "I did it!"

"Such a shame." Peashooter shook his head. "You had such potential. . . ."

"What? Are you breaking up with me or something?"

"You're trying to take away my Tribe."

"What are you talking about?"

"Sorry, Spencer, but I can't have members of my own clan contradicting me. *You're a traitor to your own kind and not loyal to us.*"

Before I knew what he was up to, Peashooter kicked my foot off the grid.

I wobbled for a second before my shoulder landed on the fiberglass panel.

I was lying on a flimsy two-foot-by-four-foot sheet of acoustic tile.

I felt the fiberglass beneath my belly begin to sag.

I heard the tile crack.

Oh boy.

"Been nice knowing you, Spencer."

If it hadn't been for Martin Mendleson cushioning my fall, I would've broken a bone or two. Lucky for me, his shoulders absorbed the bulk of my impact before I landed on the linoleum.

Dust and fiberglass particles snowed through the air as Mr. Rorshuck's math class surrounded me. None looked more stunned than Rorshuck himself, a blossom of saliva-soaked notebook paper blooming on his forehead.

"This isn't the way to the bathroom," I said.

I took a quick puff off of My Little Friend. Once I got my breath back, I looked up to the ceiling.

Peashooter was gone.

LEAVE
OF
ABSENCE

could blow their cover right now, I thought as I awaited my death sentence in Pritchard's office. I could lead Pritchard down to the boiler room, show him where the Tribe has been hiding this entire time, and in a blink, this underground ring of runaways would be broken up for good.

But my beef wasn't with the Tribe.

Just Peashooter.

He had turned the Tribe into the embodiment of the very attitudes they'd rallied against.

He knew I could rat him and the rest out.

But why take the risk?

Because without the Tribe, I have no friends.

Because my teachers don't believe a word I say.

Because even my mom thinks I'm crazy.

I've got no one.

I had spent all this time trying to get in with the most

exclusive clique at Greenfield. And my membership had been officially revoked.

How am I going to crawl my way out of this one?

"Give me one good reason," Pritchard said, storming in. "I'm sincerely asking you for just one simple reason why I should believe anything you say right now."

"You've got nothing to lose?"

"Not good enough."

"I've got everything to lose?"

"At least tell me you read the book." He exhaled. "Can you do that for me?"

The question caught me off guard. "What book?"

"*The Catcher in the Rye?*"

"Not . . . yet?"

Pritchard shrank. It looked liked I'd hurt his feelings.

"But it's at the top of my reading list, I swear!" I said.

"Consider this strike two."

"Can't we just say it was a foul ball?"

Before I could dig my own grave any deeper, Pritchard's attention shifted behind me. I turned . . .

". . . Mom?" I said. "What are you doing here?"

"Mrs. Pendleton—please, come in." Pritchard waved her in. "Thank you for joining us on such short notice. We were just about to discuss Spencer's suspension."

• • •

Three days' suspension. Three days at home.

To reflect on what I'd done.

Mom wouldn't talk to me during our drive home. Her knuckles were turning white from gripping the steering wheel.

To fill up the silence, I tried to turn on the radio.

Mom instantly switched it off.

She laid into me. "*The ceiling*, of all places! What were you doing up there?"

"You wouldn't believe me if I told you. . . ."

"Try me! Because at this point I don't know what to believe." She started counting off example after example of me not acting like me: "You haven't been sleeping, you've got a temper you've never had before, and you don't talk to me anymore!"

I thought about the Tribe. How each one of them must've had this exact same conversation with their parents before they ran away. Maybe it helped them push on.

Could I really have disappeared into thin air and never let anyone know what happened to me?

Peashooter did. Compass did. Yardstick did. Sporkboy did.

Even Sully.

Poof. Good as ghosted.

"You ever wonder what it would be like if I wasn't around, Mom?"

"What's that supposed to mean?"

"Never mind."

Mom slammed on the brakes, and we screeched to a halt.

The car directly behind us had to brake just as fast in order to avoid puckering up to our rear fender.

Mom spun toward me. "You can't just say something like that and take it back by saying *never mind*! You're not thinking about—"

She cut herself short.

"What?"

Mom's eyes widened. Something on my shoulder caught her attention.

I looked down and—*whoops*—wouldn't you know it, but I was bleeding through the sleeve of my shirt.

Before I could stop her, Mom had pulled up my shirtsleeve.

I didn't think it was possible for her eyes to open any wider, but one look at the Tribe insignia branded into my arm and they expanded to the size of Firestone tires.

"It's not what you think, Mom. . . ."

"Did you—did you hurt yourself *on purpose*?"

"I can explain—"

Her eyes were watering up. "How could you do something like this?"

"You're not listening to me!"

"Then what? *What is it?*"

"You *really* want to hear the truth?"

"That's all I've ever asked for!"

The car behind us honked its horn.

"Fine," I sighed. "Ever since we got here, there was something strange about school."

I couldn't believe I was doing this. The others would kill me if they found out.

"At first," I kept going, "it felt like the school was haunted—"

Mom got that look on her face. It crept up into her eyes and eased into her cheeks, like she'd just eaten something sour.

I knew that look. I'd seen it a million times before.

"I'm telling you the truth! The school has people . . . living in it. Students who used to go to Greenfield but dropped out. Not *dropped out*. More like *dropped in*."

"Spencer . . ."

"The kids who never fit in. Well—they finally found a place where they do! They've made the school their home. And they asked me to join them."

The car behind us honked again, longer this time.

Mom looked like I'd said something so mean, so cruel, that she'd never be able to forgive me. "Is it so hard for you to tell me the truth?"

"See for yourself! They're there right now!"

"I don't want to hear it anymore! I've trusted you, even when the voice in the back of my head said I shouldn't—and still, *still* you try to take advantage of me!"

We both went silent. There was nothing left in either of us to yell about. It had all come flooding out from our mouths, drowning us both.

All that was left was the continuous whine of the car at our backs, blaring its horn at us.

"Maybe you'd be happier giving your father a hard time,"

she said. "Go live with him. See how long he puts up with your attitude."

"I hate you." The words were barely even a whisper, but there they were.

"You're not such fun to be around either."

• • •

I held off on slipping into the kitchen until Mom was upstairs. I lifted the phone receiver from its cradle with the kind of technical delicacy a bomb squad uses when disarming a land mine.

Nothing but a dial tone.

Perfect.

I knew his number by heart. It used to be my phone number, too. I punched in the digits without even thinking.

First ring: *Pick up the phone pick up the phone pick up the phone . . .*

Second ring: *Please pick up please pick up please . . .*

Third: *Pick up pick up pick up . . .*

"Hello?" The voice on the other end sounded unsure of who would be calling.

"Dad?"

"Hey, bud . . ." Instant warmth. The tone of his voice softened in milliseconds. Suddenly he was Dad again. "Whatcha up to?"

"Oh, you know. Nothing much, really. How 'bout you?"

"Little of this, little of that."

It sounded like he was doing something else while talking to me. I found myself feeling instantly jealous over whatever Activity #2 was.

"Your mother still giving you a hard time?"

"You know how she is . . . always worried I'm gonna burn something down."

"Tell her I said hey. Better yet—*don't*."

"Okay."

"Sounds like something's on your mind. . . ."

"Just miss you, is all."

"Miss you too, bud."

"You—you think we could get together? Just you and me?"

"You bet."

"Really?"

"Sure thing," he said. "I'm a little tied up at the moment— but I bet we could hang, say, at the end of the month. How's that sound?"

"The end of the month?"

"You know how busy things get this time of year. One week. Two weeks, *tops*—okay? Christmas is coming up, so I want you to start thinking of something you can't live without. Something expensive. Just don't go burning down any more buildings between now and then, okay? Now, I should get off the phone before *tu madre* wants to talk. . . ."

"Okay."

"Talk soon, bud."

Just as he hung up, I blurted out, "Love you, Dad—"

Nothing but dial tone purring in my ear.

The second I plopped the phone onto its cradle, I felt this knot twist in my stomach.

"What'd he say?"

I spun around—and sure enough, there was Mom, leaning her head against the door frame. She didn't seem angry at me for calling him. Just kind of . . . *nothing*.

"He's not coming, is he?" she asked.

"No."

MEAT THE PARENTS

Sully had no idea I was doing this. Standing at the door to what was once her house. About to ring her bell.

I didn't know what to expect next. All I knew was my lungs suddenly decided to go on strike. I fumbled for My Little Friend and gulped a gust of chest steroids.

"Can I help you?"

A man with a twenty-o'clock shadow peered from behind the chain-locked gap in the doorway. A comb hadn't plowed through his hair in days. Maybe even weeks.

I'd recognize that hair anywhere.

Sully had her father's locks.

"Is this the Tulliver residence?"

"Yes?"

"Are you . . . Sully's dad?"

"Who are you?"

"A friend. Of Sully's."

"You're just in time." He unlatched the chain-lock. "There's been another occurrence."

"Um . . . occurrence?"

"She's back!"

. . .

The house was so quiet, I couldn't tell if I was hearing a clock ticking away in some corner of the house, or if my own pulse was slowing to a dull trudge.

Where was *Mrs.* Tulliver?

A stillness hung over the room as if the air refused to move.

This house needed an inhaler.

"Have a seat," Mr. Tulliver said. "She should be returning shortly."

"I can't really stay for long. . . ."

"*Please*. We need to be still. She won't manifest if there's any interference."

First thing I noticed were the pictures.

Sully's face was framed all across the walls. Photographs of Sully as a little girl at the beach, her auburn hair pulled back.

Sully as a baby in her mother's arms.

Sully just before she disappeared.

I shouldn't be here. This was a bad idea.

"How did you say you knew Sully?" he asked.

He said *knew*. Not *know*. Past tense.

"From school," I said. "I know her from school. *Knew* her from school."

"Sully didn't talk a lot about her friends. After her mother passed away, she didn't spend much time with kids her age."

"We've only met recently."

"*Recently?* I knew it!" He clapped his hands. "Of course she'd establish contact with one of her old friends! You two were close, then, yes?"

"I guess you could say that. . . ."

I suddenly noticed the deep rings under his eyes.

He looked like he was being haunted.

"I pushed her away—I know that now. She took care of me when I should've been taking care of her. I treated her like an adult—not a child—so it's understandable that she'd reach out to someone her own age first."

Against all better judgment on my part, I went ahead and said, "Not that I know anything, Mr. Tulliver, but if I were you . . ."

"Yes?"

Deep breath. "Don't give up on her just yet."

He seemed to ponder this for a bit, allowing the room to go silent again.

"The worst part was never knowing where she was," he eventually said. "Whether she was alive or dead. But it was only *after* I had accepted the fact that now she was with her mother that she came *back* to me. Sully's finally come home. . . ."

He thought she was dead.

"She's everywhere in this house," he continued. "I'll pass her room and hear her giggling behind the door. I'll walk by the bathroom and hear her turn off the faucet. I'll even hear her walking along the hallway upstairs while I'm down here. . . ."

Mr. Tulliver wasn't haunted by the ghost of Sully.

He was being haunted by the *memory* of her.

He nodded to me. "If we wait here long enough, she'll come back again. We just have to be patient. You'll see."

The clock in my chest started chiming off a series of steady heart attacks: *Ding! Ding! Ding!*

I bolted up from my chair. "I'm really sorry to have bothered you, sir—"

"What did Sully say to you?"

"I really should be going," I said, rushing for the front door.

"Please, *please*—just do me one favor."

I stopped.

"Tell her . . . tell her that I'm sorry."

FORTY DETAINED DAYS/FORTY SUSPENDED NIGHTS

I never thought I'd feel this way, but I really needed to get back to school.

There was some unfinished business to attend to.

Peashooter had gone too far. He was taking quotes from his favorite books and warping the words to fit what he wanted to say. He had convinced the rest of the Tribe to believe in him, that his way was the right way, *the only way*—but now that I'd seen the familial aftershocks of his manipulation firsthand, tearing these parents apart, I knew I had to stop him.

I just had to figure out how.

How can one kid stand up to a nose-pierced Napoleon?

I had two days left on my suspension to come up with a plan.

I was in my bedroom holding the copy of *The Catcher in the Rye* Pritchard had given me. Calling it a *book* was misleading. The plain white cover was holding on for dear life, and the spine had given out long ago. The only thing keeping the pages together was a rubber band.

Since I was on lockdown, I wasn't leaving my room—so I decided to see what Pritchard had been talking about all this time.

A passage around page 188 struck a nerve:

"The mark of an immature man is that he wants to die nobly for a cause, while the mark of a mature man is that he wants to live humbly for one."

I reread the sentence again, out loud this time.

I looked at Sully's photocopied MISSING flyer thumbtacked to my wall.

ME: *What do you think Salinger's getting at?*

SULLY: *Heck if I know. You're reading the book, not me. I'm just a voice in your head.*

ME: *You're a big help, Sully. Thanks a lot.*

SULLY: *Maybe he's saying that an immature man wants to die in the line of fire because that will get him all the attention— but what then? He's dead. A lot of good that does for the cause. But a mature man realizes that the true sign of strength is to live and fight for what you believe in every day, day after day. The cause is greater than the man. . . .*

ME: *Oh. Yeah—that's what I was going to say too.*

SULLY: *Sure you were, Spencer, . . . sure you were.*

What was Pritchard up to? Did he want me to see something of myself in this Caulfield character?

By the time Mom knocked on my door, I had nearly finished reading the whole book. "Didn't you hear me calling?"

"Just got wrapped up in my reading, I guess. . . ."

"Dinner's getting cold."

•••

That night, I made a list of all the books and short stories and plays Peashooter was fond of using on the rest of the Tribe:

Lord of the Flies. White Fang. The Call of the Wild. The Outsiders. "The Most Dangerous Game." *The Art of War. All's Well that Ends Well.* "The Pit and the Pendulum." *The Red Badge of Courage.*

I had some brushing up to do.

And less than two days to do it.

When I returned to school, I knew Peashooter would be waiting for me. Bic guns a-blazing. He would come at me with everything the Tribe had.

There was no way he'd let this go. Not with what I knew— like the location of their hideout and their true identities.

I was the Student Who Knew Too Much.

But I wasn't going down without a fight. If Peashooter wanted a war, fine.

To the law of claw and fang!

THE
BOOB IN
BOOBY TRAP

om drove me to school for my first day back. No kiss on the forehead this time.

"Remember your inhaler?"

"Forgot it," I said. "Don't worry—I've got a spare in my locker."

I looked out the window toward Greenfield. The building had been given a yuletide face-lift since I'd left. It was completely covered in tinsel and Christmas colors.

There was no telling what was waiting for me inside.

"Any words of wisdom for me? Sure could use some right about now."

"Don't rock the boat, Spencer. *Ever* again."

"No more boat-rocking from me, Mom."

I'm sinking this ship.

• • •

Time for the final showdown.

Pushing through Greenfield's front doors, I felt like a cowboy ready to square off in a duel.

Cue the harmonica sound track.

Cue tumbleweeds.

It felt like all eyes were on me the second I entered. As soon as I stared back, catching any one of these werekids by the eyeball, they'd bow their head and step aside.

Who knew what I might do next? As far as my classmates were concerned, I was Public (Education) Enemy #1. There was no telling what I was capable of.

Everybody cleared a path as I ambled through the hall. I heard a few whispers—*the newbie's back, what's he up to?*—but I kept rambling.

There was only one person under this school's roof that I was looking for.

But first—a little detour to my locker.

I needed to reload.

When I popped open the plastic cap and brought My Little Friend up to my lips, I glanced down just in time to see segmented legs crawling out of the mouthpiece.

There was a spider hiding inside my inhaler.

A spider. Inside. My inhaler.

And not just any kind of spider, either:

A black widow.

Another inch and that arachnid would've gone right down my windpipe.

Sully was the etymologist, but this had Peashooter's dirty fingerprints all over it.

I flung my third lung to the floor and—*SQUISH.*

Instant black jam.

You're going down, Peashooter. I don't care if I have to take the rest of the school down with me, but this ends today. . . .

Now, where was he?

• • •

The boiler room was empty.

No trace of the Tribe.

Every last book, every last weapon from their arsenal of modified school supplies, every last bit of tribal graffiti on the walls—*all gone.*

They must've known I'd come looking for evidence. Something, *anything*, that could prove their existence.

Somebody must have cleaned up after them.

"What are you doing down here?"

I spun around to discover Pritchard standing behind me, arms crossed at his chest.

"You're tailing me?" I asked.

"Considering it's your first day back, I figured I should keep an eye on you."

"No need to roll out the welcome wagon for me, sir."

"In my office. *Now.*"

• • •

Apparently, *somebody* had checked out over two dozen books under my name, then ripped out every page and flushed them down the toilets in the boys' bathroom.

What is Peashooter up to?

"I haven't even set foot in the library."

"I'm not stupid," Pritchard said, in his office. "I know it couldn't have been you."

"*Finally!* Somebody believes me."

"But I know you know who the culprit is." Pritchard's voice dropped an octave. "Tell me who they are, and you'll be absolved."

Deep breath. "That's okay, sir."

"Spencer . . . I can understand how you might think protecting them is the right thing to do—but trust me, it's not."

I could end all this right now. Here's my chance. . . .

"Think I'm fine handling this on my own, but thanks, Jim."

"Please. Stop calling me Jim."

"After all we've been through together?"

"Just get back to class. And don't let me catch you nosing around the basement again."

Pritchard escorted me out of his office. Passing the front desk, a microphone caught my eye.

The school's PA system.

This is where Pritchard sits and makes his announcements every day, his voice reaching into each classroom.

There were only three steps between me and the mic.

Now or never.

Before Pritchard knew what I was up to, I bolted for the PA system and flipped the switch. A peel of feedback screeched over the intercom.

"Hey—*Peashooter*!" I heard myself say, my voice echoing throughout the entire school. "I know you can hear me. I'm coming for you. Why don't you stop hiding and face me like a real—"

Pritchard killed the switch before I could finish. The rumble of my voice halted.

"Spencer!"

I booked it out of the office.

"Sorry, sir!"

Pritchard chased after me, but once I was in the hallway, I could hear his voice fade. "Spencer, get back here. . . ."

No turning back now.

I'd gone rogue.

• • •

Simms didn't hear me enter the boys' room. He was too busy extracting paper from the toilet.

"Thought I'd find you here," I said.

Simms glanced over his shoulder, acting not all too surprised to find me standing behind him. He reached his gloved hand in and pulled out a soggy clump of paper.

"Somebody's really got it out for you today."

"What are they up to?" I asked.

"Who?"

"You know who. What is Peashooter going to do?"

Mr. Simms held up a page torn out from some book. He read: "*The facts of life took on a fiercer aspect; and while he faced that aspect uncowed, he faced it with all the latent cunning of his nature aroused.*"

"That's from *The Call of the Wild*," I said.

Simms smiled.

"This is one of my favorite books. I remember reading it way back when." He closed his eyes and recited, "*. . . the blood lust, the joy to kill—all this was Buck's. . . .*"

When he said "this," he held out his hands and motioned to the walls surrounding him. For a second, listening to Simms, it sure sounded like he was referring to school.

Our school.

I recited along with him. "*. . . to kill with his own teeth and wash his muzzle to the eyes in warm blood!*"

Just then, all the fiberglass panels shattered over our heads.

Peashooter, Yardstick, Compass, and Sporkboy dropped down from the ceiling. They were wearing matching brown sweatshirts with the hoods pulled over their heads.

An incognito assault during school hours.

No Sully, though.

Where is she?

"Mr. Simms!" I tried warning him. "Watch out! They're—"

I cut myself off.

Nobody moved. Nobody even breathed.

All this time I'd thought Peashooter was the leader of the pack.

Turns out I was wrong.

"You're . . . one of them, aren't you?"

Simms nodded.

"Turn around," he said. "It's probably best if you didn't see this. . . ."

I took an arachnid-free gasp of air from My Little Friend and turned toward the bathroom mirror.

"See you around, Spence," Peashooter said.

I caught Sporkboy's reflection as he brought a corn dog down on top of my head. The blunt thud of a half-frozen nunchuck knocked me out cold.

GHOST STORY
NUMBER SIX:
MR. SIMMS

The smell of ammonia woke me. Coming to, I found myself in small room surrounded by shelves filled with industrial-size bottles of cleaning agents.

The janitor's closet.

There was a cot in the corner. Blankets. Yellowed yearbooks. Brittle pictures of kids from decades ago. Somebody had obviously been living in here.

Mr. Simms. His life intermingled with cleaning supplies.

I struggled up to my feet. Looking down at myself, I realized I was wearing a brown hoodie. The hood was already pulled over my head. I performed a quick pat down of the cowl, discovering a pair of antlers sewn on top.

Antlers?

"Welcome back to the land of the living."

I spun around to find Simms holding a yearbook in his hand.

"How long was I out?"

"Not that long."

I took a step back. "Are you going to kill me now?"

Simms shook his head, laughing. "Nobody's going to hurt you."

"Tell that to Peashooter."

"Here," he said. "I want to show you something. . . ."

The yearbook hadn't been opened in so long, a nest of book lice had settled in its spine. I cracked the cover and watched them shower out from between the pages.

The photographs had yellowed. The faded faces of each student looked like jaundiced zombies.

But there he was, hidden on page 37.

"I ended up running away from home shortly after that picture was taken," he told me. "That's the last photo of me *ever*."

Timothy Simms.

Sixth grade.

"I was the kind of kid who always got in trouble," he continued. "One day I just decided I wanted to get in trouble somewhere other than school. Spent the next few years of my life on the road, wandering around. Only, when I finally came home, there wasn't anything left. No family. No friends. All gone."

"So, what did you do?"

"Started looking around for familiar things," he said. "Anything that reminded me of who I used to be."

That's how he found his way back to Greenfield.

"I remembered school. So I wondered if school would remember me."

Turns out it didn't.

The faces were different. The teachers he knew were all gone. Nothing felt familiar to him anymore.

"The school needed to bulk up its custodial staff," he said. "I asked if they were hiring, and the very next day, I had myself a job mopping up these halls."

Everyone called him Mr. Simms, if they called him anything at all. And the only reason anyone ever called on him was if something needed cleaning.

Nobody paid attention to him.

Not the students.

Not the administration.

Not the teachers.

Not unless there was a mess.

He was a ghost to these people. A living, breathing ghost. He haunted the halls of Greenfield Middle during school hours, in broad daylight.

"I'd end up spending the night sometimes," he said. "Had a cot set up in the back room here, out of everybody's way. I'd sleep for a few hours, then start my day up again before anybody else even set foot in the building."

The cafeteria ladies would slip him a sandwich after the students had their lunch. He would sift through the lost-and-found for clothes.

Weeks would go by and he would barely step outside the building.

"Nobody knew I was living here," he said. "*I* didn't even know I was living here."

Years later, Mr. Simms was setting up his cot in the janitor's closet one night—when, from over his head, he heard a shifting sound. He pulled back the fiberglass paneling and discovered a pair of tennis shoes scuttling away from him.

"I grabbed an ankle and dragged this boy out. He struggled, but I held onto him."

Peashooter. He saw Mr. Simms's domestic spread. Junk from the lost-and-found accumulating in piles. Books nobody wanted to read. Clothes people had thrown out.

Mr. Simms had created a home for himself—and Peashooter was his first houseguest.

"The boy asked me if he was in trouble," he said. "Funny thing was, I was gonna ask him the same question about me!"

Mr. Simms didn't say anything about Peashooter's exploration of the building, and Peashooter didn't say anything about Mr. Simms's home away from no-home.

Then, one day, Peashooter brought a friend along: Compass.

"Sorta just started out like that," Mr. Simms said. "There were three of us. Then four. Looking after them was no big deal, no matter how rambunctious they get. Boys will be boys. . . ."

Whether he knew it or not, he had been the first.

The original member.

The chief.

"Sure felt like family to me." He smiled. "Hadn't had one of them for a long time."

Listening to Simms, a thought popped into my head: *You don't get to pick your family—but sometimes, your family picks you.*

I really missed my real family just then.

Sully, too.

"It's a shame," Simms said. "I know they all really liked you. Even Peashooter."

"I find that hard to believe."

"We all saw the potential in you. Me, most of all. I was the one who suggested that they let you join. Too bad it didn't work out."

"So . . . what happens now?"

"Just sit tight until after the assembly."

"*Assembly?* What assembly?"

"The holiday concert. We can't have you crashing the party, now, can we?"

Mr. Simms slipped through the closet door. I heard a click from the other side before I could rush. *Locked.*

No getting out the easy way.

I did a drum solo with my fists against the door.

"Hey! Is anyone out there? *Heeeeeeelp!*"

Whatever the Tribe was up to, I knew it wasn't going to be good. Peashooter needed me out of the picture long enough to set me up. Simms would let me out of this broom closet only after the damage was done, leaving me to take the fall for them.

Quick. Think fast.

Should I make a Molotov cocktail out of a bottle of bleach and burn my way out?

Bleach doesn't burn.

I looked up to the ceiling. Toward the fiberglass panels just above my head. The acoustic tiles were about six inches out of reach from the top of the closet's shelf.

Okay. I can do this.

I think I can do this.

I hope I can do this.

There are heroes—and then there are men. Men get called to action because their fellow classmates need help. *Heroes* you see on TV, with capes and bulletproof bodies. They aren't real. *Men* never have cameras trained on them when they save the day. They don't get the fawning admiration of the masses or hot groupies. Not at all.

Time to man up, Spencer. . . .

I climbed up the nearest shelving unit until it began to buckle under my weight.

Take it slow. Steady, Spencer. . . .

Soon there was only one shelf left. Bottles of cleaning agents wobbled. The shelves' center of gravity was thrown out of whack, thanks to all my King Kong-ing.

Stop. Hold still. Get your balance.

I reached my arm up, my fingers just barely grazing the fiberglass. There was no more leverage.

Just a few more millimeters . . .

A bottle of bleach rolled off the top shelf and burst open on the floor. Then a bottle of ammonia.

The fumes filled up the room in seconds. My eyes began to burn and I started to feel light-headed.

This is bad. This is all very, very bad.

I reached my arm up over my head. The shelf began to tip. More bottles of ammonia were suddenly dive-bombing their way down to the floor, turning the janitor's closet into one big gas chamber. I could feel my chest filling up with noxious toxins.

My Little Friend to the rescue!

I fished my inhaler from my sweatshirt and slipped the mouthpiece between my teeth. I took a deep puff.

I lunged for the ceiling, sending the shelving unit smashing against the ground. The panel popped open, leaving me dangling, legs kicking.

It took all my strength just to lift myself into the ceiling.

Made it! I'm in.

I took another puff off My Little Friend and caught my breath.

Steady now. Take it slow. Balance your weight. No fast movements.

As I crawled, I tried to take my mind off the fact that any infinitesimal shift could send me crashing into a classroom below.

I am light as a feather. . . .

I am a leaf on the breeze. . . .

I am the wings of a butterfly. . . .

How far had I gone? I had to have been halfway across the

school by now. It was so dark up there, I couldn't tell.

Something softened underneath my belly. I heard a crackle.

I am light as a feather. . . .

I am a leaf on the breeze. . . .

I am the wings of a butterfly. . . .

That's when the ceiling collapsed under me.

Again.

THE TROJAN REINDEER

I landed in the cafeteria just as Assistant Principal Pritchard's voice crackled over the intercom, inviting students to the gym for our ChristmasKwanzaHanukahLasPosadas holiday concert.

Classrooms emptied into the hallway as all five hundred and thirty-six students attending Greenfield Middle were corralled in the gymnasium.

Remember: *Five hundred and thirty-six students.*

There will be a quiz later.

One location. Tight confinements. The entire student body all gathered together.

This can't be good.

The seventh-grade choristers were crooning "Here Comes Santa Claus" when I burst into the gym: "Bells are ringing, children singing, all is merry and bright, so hang your stockings and say your prayers . . ."

. . . because you're all about to get attacked by a wild pack of middle-school dropouts.

It felt like I had entered a winter-wonder wilderness. Silver Mylar icicles dangled overhead. Vines of Christmas-colored crepe paper overwhelmed the basketball nets. Strings of Christmas-tree lights crept along the walls, blinking like radioactive berries.

Pritchard, decked out in full-blown Santa wear, was *ho-ho-ho*-ing through the gym atop a sled mounted on wheels, pulled by a batch of students dressed in the exact same hoodies that I was wearing, complete with sewn-on antlers.

Our cheerleading squad pranced across the basketball court, done up like Santa's little helpers, with pointy ears and red and green tights bedazzled with jingle bells.

Every step sounded like a million tiny dinner bells.

And leading the whole procession, rather than Rudolph the Red-Nosed mascot, was our very own trusted Griz the Grizzly.

That's it!

Sporkboy was in the costume again, with a Peashooter-Donner, Yardstick-Blitzen, and Compass-Comet close behind.

No time to second guess myself. Time to act. And fast.

I rushed the basketball court, shouting at the top of my lungs, "Don't go near the reindeer! Don't go near the reindeer!"

The music halted. The singing stopped. All of the students, all of Santa's little cheerleaders, even the reindeer themselves turned toward me as I yelled my head off.

"It's a setup! Get away from Griz! Get away from Griz!"

Leaping through the air, I tackled our school's mascot.

The two of us tumbled to the ground, rolling over each other in front of the entire wolf pack of werekids.

"Get off of me!" the muffled voice from inside the grizzly snarled. "Get off!"

"Let's see you ruin Christmas now, Sporkboy!"

Griz swatted his clawed paws at my face. "What are you doing?!"

I grabbed hold and tore the bear's fuzzy head clear off his shoulders, and raised his mask above my head in a gesture of victorious stuffed-animal decapitation. *"Ah-ha!"*

I looked down to see Martin Mendleson between my knees. *Whoops.*

"What is wrong with you?" he yelled. "Have you gone completely mental?!"

Each reindeer pulled back their horned hoodies, revealing not Peashooter, not Yardstick, not Compass, but three wide-eyed sixth graders, looking at me like I was some kind of rabid holiday-party crasher about to attack them next.

Well . . . this is a little embarrassing.

"But you're not . . ."

I wanted to pull the drawstrings on my sweatshirt and hide under my hoodie.

"But . . ."

Like the saying goes: *When you assume* . . .

So what was the Tribe's plan?

Their *real* plan?

"Mr. Pendleton," Assistant Principal Pritchard growled from beneath his white beard, his cheeks burning cranberry-sauce red, "get to my office *this instant!*"

Before I could respond, the overhead lights snuffed out. The murmur of students flitted through the pitch blackness.

"*Here was a gorgeous triumph.*" Peashooter's voice beckoned over the gymnasium speakers: "*They were missed; they were mourned; hearts were breaking on their account; tears were being shed; accusing memories of unkindness to these poor lost lads were rising up, and unavailing regrets and remorse were being indulged; and best of all, the departed were the talk of the whole school. . . .*"

I'm pretty sure Mark Twain originally said "town" rather than "school."

I totally remember reading that chapter from *The Adventures of Tom Sawyer*—how he and Huck had staged their deaths and attended their own funerals.

Rough translation:

It wasn't until we disappeared that people even realized we existed. Now that we're gone, our classmates might realize just how cruel they'd been to us when we were still around. Better not forget us. Who we are.

So here was a little something to remember them by. . . .

A spotlight burst through the gymnasium, hitting Yardstick, who was standing at center court wearing his sweatshirt. The hood was pulled over his head, hiding the upper half of his face from the audience. All you could see was his smile. He stood with the poise of a master magician about to bowl the crowd over.

"For my first trick," he called out, "I'll need a volunteer from the audience. . . ."

Up went Yardstick's arms, holding them out at his shoulders.

"How about . . . *everybody?*"

What looked like a dozen corn dogs were suddenly launched from Yardstick's sleeves. He conducted the flow of processed-meat projectiles. *"Ta-da!"*

The entire gymnasium was immediately overwhelmed by a blitz of breaded missiles that streaked through the air before bursting over the audience.

I looked around and spotted a reindeer hiding beside the bleachers, lighting wicks and sending even more corn-dog rockets hissing into the air. I think it was Sporkboy. The Tribe was starting to blur together. I was beginning to understand that this was precisely the point. With no lights, and Tribe members wearing similar-looking sweatshirts, nobody would be able to tell for sure who was who.

One might even mistake them all for one person.

Me.

Just what Peashooter had wanted. Now, that's some real sleight-of-hand magic.

Somebody grabbed my shoulder.

Spinning around, I discovered Sully. She was wearing the same hoodie as the rest.

"You look like you've seen a ghost," she said.

"Think I have."

Sully took my hand and brought it up to her face, pressing it to her cheek.

"No ghosts here," she said. "Come with me."

"Where are we going? What's going on?"

"Trust me—you won't want to be here when it happens."

• • •

We snuck under the bleachers, maneuvering through the bubble-gum-studded framework.

"Where have you been?" I asked. "I've been looking every-where for you."

"In the lost-and-found, I guess."

"Good thing I found you!"

She wasn't smiling. "We're leaving."

"*Leaving?* Where?"

"I can't say. I'm not even supposed to be here right now."

"But—"

"Sully!" Peashooter poked his hoodied-head through the bleacher seats. "What's going on? *What're you doing with him?*"

I grabbed Sully's shoulders. "Don't," I said. "Don't leave."

Peashooter climbed down and took Sully by the arm. "We've got to go—*now!*"

Ignoring him, I said to Sully, "I met your dad."

Her face went whiter than white.

"My . . . dad?"

"He told me about your mother."

"You ratted us out—*to a parent*?" Peashooter hissed, the paper clip piercing his nose twitching like the metallic whiskers on a robotic rabbit. "I told you he was a traitor!"

"Don't listen to him," I said.

"*All the world will be your enemy,* Sully," Peashooter said. "*Whenever they catch you, they will kill you.*"

Cheap shot, but two can play that game.

"Don't think I don't know you just mangled *Watership Down*!" I went ahead and finished the quote before Peashooter could— "*But first, they have to catch you—digger, listener, runner, Sully with the swift warning!*"

Peashooter's eyes widened. His mouth opened, then quickly closed.

"What?" I asked. "You didn't think I'd bone up on my tribal required reading list? Want me to keep going? I can. *Be cunning and full of tricks, and your people will never be destroyed!*"

Fire with fire.

Books with books.

"This isn't over between you and me," Peashooter shouted. "Not by a long shot! You're dead, Spencer! *Dead!*"

Maybe I had simply hit my boiling point. Maybe I was flustered from trying to prove myself over and over again.

Maybe sometimes words aren't enough.

Whatever it was, before I even knew what I was doing, my hand sprung up from my side and pinched Peashooter by his piercing. With one swift tug, my hand came back down—with a paper clip between my fingers.

Did I just do that?

Peashooter cupped his nose and howled. He fell to his knees.

Sully looked at me with a mixture of happiness and sadness, anger and confusion.

"Your father misses you." I couldn't bring myself to tell her how haunted he was. "It's not too late to come home."

"The Tribe needs me. They are my home."

"Sully—"

She grabbed the bleeding Peashooter by the arm and yanked him up from the floor, dragging him away.

"Sully—*wait.*"

I could feel my throat constricting. My chest was getting heavy, another asthma attack brewing in my lungs. I pulled out My Little Friend and took a quick gust off that medicated crap, bringing my breathing back.

As soon as I pulled it from my lips, there was Sully, pressing hers against mine.

We were kissing. It definitely constituted kissing.

There was a vague taste of ChapStick on Sully's lips, a ghost flavor of strawberries haunting her mouth.

"I'm sorry. . . ."

She took one step away from me, then two. Then twenty.

Then a million.

It felt like the bleachers had begun to shut on their own while I was standing beneath them, slamming closed on my chest.

My ribs.

My heart.

I wanted the risers to seal me in like a coffin, bury me below the student body of Greenfield.

Sully was gone.

• • •

I crawled out from the bleachers and watched the last of the fried fire-porks display. The bottle-dogs kept exploding in a sparkling yellow mist of gunpowdered cornmeal, showering across the crowd.

Rather than run, the students *oohed* and *aahed* like this was all part of the show.

Seemed like everybody was actually having some fun at an assembly for once.

Yardstick conducted one more round into the air.

Suddenly it all made sense.

This was Yardstick's talent show.

This was Sporkboy's lunch.

This was Peashooter's official last laugh.

So what about Compass? Was this his long-lost science fair project?

As the last bits of cornmeal dissipated into the air, I realized Yardstick had vanished. So had Sporkboy.

Pritchard and his reindeer were all that was left on the basketball court.

The only hoodied hoodlum in the court was . . .

Me.

I started to wonder: *What if the corn-rockets are nothing but a distraction? A ruse used to keep everybody in their seats?*

Distraction from what?

What happened next was the real main attraction.

Pity poor Riley Callahan.

Sitting three rows back, twelve students in, he buckled over and clutched at his stomach.

"Something doesn't feel right. . . ."

All this time, I thought the attack would happen *during* the Christmas concert.

Turns out the attack had already taken place.

Good thing I'd missed lunch today.

The cafeteria ladies had gotten into the holiday spirit and served a meal of mashed potatoes, tissue-thin turkey slices, and a golf ball of stuffing, slathering it all up with a fine film of luke-warm gravy.

A quick science lesson for everybody: food poisoning happens in schools all the time. Eat a bit of, say, *contaminated cranberry sauce*, it'll incubate in your belly until it's off to the hospital for you. Symptoms include *abdominal cramping, nausea, vomiting, diarrhea.*

Nobody knew that better than Compass.

What could infect an entire school's worth of students all at once?

Mushrooms.

Just like the kind Compass had asked me to pick for him from the soccer field.

What had he called them? Amanita mascara-something-or-other. He said the fungus was highly psycho-hyper-active. Whatever that meant.

Oh boy.

The interval between lunch and the concert was all the time everybody's stomach needed to get this party started. And in case the gestation period varied from tummy to tummy, Compass had come up with a catalyst to kick-start a school-wide heave-ho:

The overwhelmingly meaty aroma of burned corn dogs.

Riley abruptly trumpeted a low C from below, his inverted burp heralding the prelude to a flatulent symphony.

I heard another whistle, shriller than Riley's, like a piccolo squeaking through the air from a few rows farther back.

And another.

Before long, an entire cluster of kids became the broken-wind section for a methane-fueled orchestra, performing a full-blown acoustical salute to air pollution.

I swore I heard a backside bassoon.

A colonic clarinet.

A farting flute.

The rumblings of the most odoriferous earthquake were passing through the gym, hitting a 7.9 on the Richter scale. You would've sworn a gas main had broken beneath the bleachers, belching out a cloud of noxious fumes and turning our gym into one big airborne toxic event.

At first, everybody thought it was funny to listen to this sliding scale of backdoor bagpiping. Students were hitting every note imaginable from behind—and for those who hadn't begun, they were cracking up. But the quickest way to quit snickering over your neighbor's uncontrollable tailwind was to commence letting 'em rip yourself.

And as every student of musical (de)composition knows, *What begins with the woodwinds, must eventually move on to the brass.*

Pity poor Sarah Haversand.

"I don't feel so . . ."

Before she could finish, she puked directly on the student sitting in front of her. That student just so happened to be none other than Riley Callahan.

A blossom of vomit spread over Riley's unsuspecting head. Little dribbles of cranberry sauce trickled down his temples. He had just started to grow his hair back, and now it was buried beneath a soup of partially digested Christmas-ized cafeteria food.

Riley responded with his stomach suddenly pumping out its contents, vomiting onto the cloned Cro-Magnon crony sitting just next to him.

And then that Cro-Magnon barfed on the boy just next to him.

And he puked on her and she puked on him and he puked on her and . . .

You get the idea.

In the spirit of "the show must go on," our school's choral group attempted to warble through "White Christmas."

Ever heard a chorus of choristers puking in unison? It's a perfect pitch of *do re mi* mixed in with *urp ech hyuck.* A whole new upchucked Christmas carol:

"I'm dream-ing of a whi-ite Christ-maaaaulch . . ."

"Just like the ones I used to meaaaaach . . ."

"Where the tree tops glisteeeeeeach . . ."

"And children listenaeeeeelch . . ."

Sarah tried to break away from the bleachers, only to fall face-first in a Slip 'N Slide of cranberry sauce. She skidded halfway across the basketball court on her stomach.

"Oh God," she wailed. "It's *everywheeeeeeeere!*"

But all that was nothing compared to what the percussion section had in store.

Ready for the grand finale?

Riley tried to stand up from the bleachers—only to freeze in midlift.

His eyes widened. Jaw dropped.

Something was happening.

Had happened.

A dam had broke, releasing a flood. His only recourse was to quickly sit back down, a bit of a squish punctuating the impact of his soggy bottom.

Riley wasn't the only one.

Other students suddenly sensed their intestines seizing and releasing, the backfire from their jumping guts just a warning shot for wetter things to come.

Now everyone was on the run(s).

I saw several cheerleaders make a break for the gym doors in hopes of beelining to the bathroom.

"Hurry up, hurry up, hurry up!"

They didn't make it.

In midstride, their desperation wilted away in leaking defeat, as they buried their faces into their soggy pom-poms and plopped onto the floor.

I couldn't help myself from imagining the entire cheerleading squad chanting:

DI-ARRHEA!

D-I-ARRHEA!

D-I-A-R-R-H-E-A!

Pity poor Martin Mendleson. He was still stuck inside his Griz costume when his butt erupted.

"Get me out of here!" he yelled. "Get me out get me out *get me ooooooooout!*"

Too late. He was essentially buried up to his neck in his own plush Porta-Potty. He waddled across the court, trapped inside the fuzzy confines of his mobile toilet. The odor drifting up from within was enough to bring tears to his eyes.

"It burns!" He clawed at his face with his paws. "It burns!"

Guess who had been left behind to conduct this symphonic fecal fiasco? This concert of Hershey squirts?

Where the Tribe had wanted revenge against Greenfield, Peashooter had only wanted revenge against me.

What was it that he said?

It's a jungle out there. . . .

Try a rain forest.

I stood by the bleachers and watched the whole calamity unfold, every last drip.

I couldn't help but feel sorry for my classmates as they wallowed in this newly spawned swampland—but then it dawned on me:

For just one brief and brilliant, slippery and stinky moment—everybody, all the jocks and cheerleaders, the bullies and the bullied, each and every last clique—was exactly the same.

Nobody was judging anyone anymore.

Right in time for the holidays.

Pritchard ran up to me, his Santa Claus beard speckled with recycled cranberry sauce.

"What's going on?" He grabbed my shoulders. "What on earth is happening?"

"Merry Christmas, sir."

HOME IS WHERE THE HEART IS (CARVED)

Strike three, Spencer," Pritchard declared as he dragged me out of the gym. "I don't need to tell you what that means."

"Extra innings?"

"Expelled."

• • •

Greenfield closed its doors immediately following the holiday "consquirt" so health inspectors could investigate the sudden outbreak of food poisoning.

Perfect cover for the Tribe to make a break for it.

I was sitting outside the principal's office waiting for Mom to arrive. All the other kids were heading home, hunched over and swaddled in their gym shorts.

From farther down the hall, I heard a rattle of keys, like Marley's ghost clattering his chains. Only one person in school had that many keys attached to his hip.

Mr. Simms rolled his mop and bucket toward the gym. As soon as we made eye contact, he stopped and sat down next to me.

Neither of us said anything for the longest time. We simply stared down the empty hall before I finally broke the silence. "Where do you think they're heading?"

"Your guess is as good as mine." He shrugged. "Lots of other schools in this district, by my count."

"How come you didn't run with them?"

"I'd only hold them back. Besides, they can take care of themselves now."

He was missing them already. I didn't blame him.

"What are you going to say to Pritchard?" he asked. "You going to tell him?"

"What? About the tribe of missing kids hiding in his school?" I shook my head.

"So you're going to take the fall for them?" Simms asked.

"Not for them. *For me*. I'm doing this for me."

And a little for Sully.

Simms smiled. "Guess Peashooter misjudged you after all. . . ."

• • •

Pritchard's office really was beginning to feel like a home away from home. But sitting there, something told me this might be my last visit.

"You really expect me to believe you're single-handedly responsible for everything that happened today?"

"Aren't I?"

"Come on, Spencer. Who are you trying to protect?"

"Just me, I swear."

"So that's your story?"

"And I'm sticking to it, sir."

"I hate to say it, but your word isn't worth that much to me right now."

"Kind of like Holden Caulfield, huh?"

Pritchard blinked. "You actually read *The Catcher in the Rye?*"

"I had a lot of time on my hands during my suspension—so yeah, I did."

"Care to share what you thought of it?"

"Well, it's like when Holden Caulfield says—"*What really knocks me out is a book that, when you're all done reading it, you wish the author that wrote it was a terrific friend of yours and you could call him up on the phone whenever you felt like it.*'"

"Good luck with that." Pritchard chuckled. "Salinger was a pretty famous recluse. After he wrote *Catcher*, he felt that people misunderstood it. They thought the book meant something that it didn't. At least not to him. So, one day, he decided to disappear."

Sounded familiar.

I wondered if Peashooter would ever pick up a copy. He'd have to infiltrate a high school to get his hands on one.

That got me thinking about the Tribe again. Which got me thinking about Sully. Which got me worrying about the whole gang out there, in the real world now, struggling to survive. *Alone.*

Why did I miss them so much?

"I wish things had turned out differently for you, Spencer," Pritchard said. "I wish we could've talked more about the book. . . ."

"Who says we can't talk now? It's not like I'm dead or anything."

"Not yet," Mom said.

She didn't look happy to see me. As soon as she stepped into Pritchard's office, she launched right in: "I don't know what to do with you anymore, Spencer. I really don't."

"I'm sorry, Mom."

"Sorry is not going to cut it."

I took a deep breath. "I know you don't believe me. I know how hard I've made things for you these last couple months. But I want you to know—I didn't mean for this to happen. Any of this. I'm not saying it wasn't my fault. It was. I'm just saying that . . . I love you, Mom. I never wanted to hurt you."

She didn't say anything for the longest time.

"I love you too, Spencer. But—"

She cut herself short. The words were having a hard time coming out of her mouth.

"But—*what*?"

She tried again. "I think it would be best if . . . for a while, at least . . . if you lived with your—"

Perfect inopportunity for Pritchard's door to open from behind me. "Sorry I'm late."

I turned around, discovering . . .

Dad.

"What did I miss?"

Everything.

• • •

My parents wanted to talk with Pritchard about my expulsion. *Privately.* So I decided to walk through Greenfield one last time.

I was still wearing the brown sweatshirt. I flipped the hoodie over my head, antlers and all, and wandered the halls.

I stepped into Mrs. Witherspoon's class. I didn't have a chance to say good-bye to her—or any of my teachers, for that matter. Not like many of them would miss me. But it was Witherspoon who got me writing about the Tribe in the first place.

I didn't have proof that the Tribe existed—but I did have their story.

Just knowing they weren't hiding in Greenfield anymore made the building feel—well, it was nothing but a school now.

I sat at my old desk and scanned the ceiling, half expecting someone to shuffle across the fiberglass panels.

But nothing. Nothing at all.

They really were gone.

Then I found it. . . .

• • •

There's a desk somewhere in Greenfield Middle School. It used to be in Mrs. Witherspoon's class, but it's probably been shuffled around to another room by now.

You just have to find it.

I did. Right where Sully had left it for me.

Hidden within all the graffiti and doodles on the desk, there is a tiny heart carved into its top. A spear pierces through the superior vena cava. The spearhead pokes out from the etched muscle's bottom chamber, a single droplet of blood dribbling off the tip.

Stretching across the left ventricle, it reads: *SULLY.*

Across the right: *SPENCE.*

And wrapping around the whole heart, it says: *FOREVER.*

Class dismissed.

Acknowledgments

Thanks to Wes Nichols, Desiree Burch, Margaret Miller, Hugo Perez, Jeffrey Dinsmore, Kyle Jarrow, Chris Steib, Lauren Cerand, Barbara Clark, Erik German, and Solana Pyne.

This book couldn't have happened without my hero Eddie Gamarra. To Ellen Goldsmith-Vein and everyone at The Gotham Group, thank you for your faith and support.

Endless thanks to Kevin Lewis. You are the punk rock Gordon Lish. Best. Editor. *Ever.* To Ricardo Mejias and the Hyperion gang, thank you for taking a chance on me.

Infinite inspiration and quotes come from Napoleon Bonaparte, *Lord of the Flies* by William Golding, *White Fang* by Jack London, *The Call of the Wild* by Jack London, *The Outsiders* by S. E. Hinton, *Watership Down* by Richard Adams, *The Catcher in the Rye* by J. D. Salinger, "The Most Dangerous Game" by

Richard Connell, *The Adventures of Tom Sawyer* by Mark Twain, *The Art of War* by Sun Tzu, *All's Well that Ends Well* by William Shakespeare, "The Pit and the Pendulum" by Edgar Allan Poe, *Johnny Tremain* by Esther Forbes, *The Red Badge of Courage* by Stephen Crane, "The Female of the Species" by Rudyard Kipling, and *Peter Pan* by J. M. Barrie.

Show me a family of readers, and I will show you
the people who move the world. . . .
—Napoleon

DON'T MISS OUT
ON YOUR NEXT TRIBAL LESSON

THE GREAT ESCAPES

Blame Martin Luther King.

Mom had to arrange my homeschooling when she realized Dad had forgotten to. I still had a semester's worth of seventh grade to survive, and she wasn't about to let me slip through the academic cracks. That meant tackling the Age of Enlightenment, square roots, and sentence structure all on my own—not to mention a whole bunch of other subjects that blurred into a chemically induced stew of misplaced integers and grammatical mistakes.

You try studying on this prescription. Class might as well have been underwater. There was a thickness to my thoughts after I popped one of these pills, slowing my synapses down. My brain had to push through sludge to reach the answers.

Fight the fog fight the fog fight the fog fight the fog . . .

But then I met Dr. King.

He was waiting for me in my history lesson. I read about how he fought for his beliefs in a nonviolent manner.

"You're telling me you stood up against injustice peacefully?" I asked. "Protest with a smile? That sort of thing?"

"*Nonviolence is a powerful and just weapon,*" he answered back from the cozy confines of my history book. "*Indeed, it is a weapon unique in history, which cuts without wounding and ennobles the man who wields it.*"

This is what happens when I study.

My books start talking back to me.

All Dad had to do was make sure I kept up with my class assignments. That usually amounted to him peaking his head into my room for a quick scan. As long as he saw a book in my hands, open and right-side up, he didn't look much further.

One night, he poked his head into my room for a quick look-see. Just as he was about to slip back out, I felt compelled to ask him—"Did you know Martin Luther King once said, '*A man who won't die for something is not fit to live*'?"

"*Sure thing.*"

"So what are you willing to die for, Dad?"

"*What's that?*"

"Nothing. Just thinking out loud."

"*Okeydoke!*"

He closed the door behind him, sealing me in with Martin. I wanted to make my room even smaller, encasing myself within my history book. Let the pages become my walls.

What was I willing to die for?

How about *who*?

I'll give you one guess.

• • •

Fifteen breakouts in the last three months alone.

Not a bad personal record, huh? When you're under house arrest, you have to find ways to stretch the ol' legs.

Of course I'd get caught. I never tampered with my ankle monitor. I kept it on, leading the police right to me.

Here are my top three breakouts of all time.

So far.

GREAT ESCAPE HALL OF FAME
ESCAPE #3: APRIL TWENTIETH
THE LOCAL LIBRARY

I had some overdue books, so I decided to hand-deliver them.

All I had was a thirty-second head start. Thirty seconds before my ankle monitor would break out into a hissy fit.

Let's break this down:

- If I ran fast enough, I could reach the end of the block in thirteen seconds.

- The next block in twenty-eight.
- The local branch of our public library was five blocks away.
- I'd have three blocks to go by the time the cops knew I was officially off the reservation.
- If we estimate that each block takes roughly twelve seconds to span, that planted me at the library's front entrance thirty-three seconds after my ankle monitor tipped Big Brother off to my whereabouts.
- Standard police response time: Two minutes, twenty-seven seconds.

My math was feeling a little fuzzy, but if my calculations were correct—I would have somewhere between one minute and fifty-seven seconds to two minutes all to myself before the authorities rolled in and dragged me away.

A bookworm can do a lot of damage with two minutes in the library.

Why not take the opportunity to peruse the newspaper archives on the Internet for sightings of feral teenagers?

Anything that might help me figure out where the Tribe had run off to.

Sully had to be out there, somewhere.

I just had to find her.

I kneeled down next to the mailbox at the edge of our yard, assuming my best sprint starting position.

Remember My Little Friend? You'd hardly even recognize

my inhaler anymore. I've "pimped my ride" since you last saw him. He now has red-and-yellow flames wrapping around the mouthpiece.

I brought him up to my lips and pumped my chest full of medicated air. Feeling my bronchioles embrace the aerosolized dose of corticosteroids, I waited for the starting pistol to fire off in my imagination and make a break for it.

On your mark . . .

Get set . . .

Go!

I'd like to go on record stating that I personally have nothing against the Greenfield County Police Department or any of its employees, particularly Officers Winston Sellars and James Cassidy. These gentlemen were only doing their job, and I have nothing but the utmost respect for them and their tireless work ethic. I wholeheartedly apologize for repeatedly putting them in the position of breaking a sweat.

You know I love you guys . . . Right?

Sellars was a squat, pug-faced patrolman, whose head barely reached his partner's shoulder. The handles on his horseshoe mustache got lost somewhere within the creases of his double chin.

Cassidy had more height and less weight. His gangly limbs left him looking like the dancing windsock you'd find outside a used-car dealership.

As soon as I saw them stumble into the library, a bit winded from their run, I flashed them a grin.

"Officers! I didn't know you had a membership to this branch. We should start our own book group."

"Time to go, Pendleton," Sellars said. "Put the book down slowly, *slowly*."

"Don't you two ever get tired of the roles society has assigned us?" I asked. "I mean, you're both Authority figures with a capital *A*. I get that. You've got this part to play, just like I do. You look at me and all you see is a Delinquent with a capital *D*, a natural born absconder—and in all fairness, I was born for the role. But don't you think maybe, *just maybe*, we can put down these clichéd designations that destiny has doomed us to fulfill and see each other not for our differences, but for our commonalities? Can't we, you know . . . just get along?"

Sellars side-glanced Cassidy.

Cassidy cleared his throat. "Let's try not to make a scene, okay?"

"Of course," I complied. "But before we go, can I recommend some reading material for your next stakeout? I just finished this book that I think you two'll love."

"What book?" Sellars asked. Cassidy elbowed him in the ribs.

"It's called *I Know Why the Caged Jailbird's Ankle Monitor Sings*," I said. "I think it's somewhere in the romance section."

Thinking quick, I tipped over a stack of romance novels waiting to be reshelved and booked it down the aisle. Sellars planted his foot on a bodice ripper, slipping on the paperback like it was a banana peel.

Cassidy was right behind me. I jumped up onto the reference

desk, leaping over a few readers' heads as I scurried across the tabletop.

Undeterred, Cassidy grabbed at my knees. I avoided his clasping hands by hopping onto the next table, making sure not to step on anybody's reading material, like some kind of clumsy ballerina dancing *en pointe*.

Cassidy sped to the end of the table, cutting me off, and I froze with one foot still hovering through the air.

Perfect arabesque.

"Get down from there, Pendleton. *Now*."

Cassidy was coming up fast. No more tables for me to scale.

The bookshelf just next to me suddenly looked a lot like a ladder.

So I started climbing.

Sellars picked himself up and followed Cassidy through the rows just below me—two mice maneuvering about a maze—as I leapt from one bookcase to the next.

"You are not lab rats," I belted out with each leap. "There is no cheese waiting at the end of this labyrinth! You're all free! Free to think for yourselves! Free to live your lives the way you want to! Freedom! *Freeeeeeedom!*"

I was running out of bookshelves. Only one more to go before I hit the wall.

But I was going for the gold here.

Or a window. Whichever came first.

I launched off the shelf with enough force to inadvertently

send the bookcase beneath me tipping over in the opposite direction.

I went one way, the shelf went another.

Once I landed on the last bookcase, I quickly spun around to behold the horrifying sight of the ledge I'd just left toppling into the neighboring case.

And the next.

Books slid off their shelves, their covers flapping haplessly through the air like flightless chickens falling to the floor as the chain reaction gained momentum.

All I could do was watch in shock as each shelf collided with the case beside it, one after another, sending patrons and police officers clearing the aisles.

I had unintentionally invented a new sporting event:

Library dominoes.

GREAT ESCAPE HALL OF FAME
ESCAPE #2: APRIL THIRTIETH
GREENFIELD MIDDLE SCHOOL

Is it my fault Doc Lobotomy never asked *which* bathroom I planned on using?

So what if I'd picked one from my old alma mater?

I knew it was a big no-no, coming back to Greenfield Middle—but I needed to see someone.

Mr. Simms's face blanched as soon as he opened the janitor's closet and discovered me inside, waiting among the shelves of cleaning fluids.

"Good lord, son," he said. "How long have you been in here?"

I knew my police escorts were on their way, so I didn't waste any time with chitchat. "Have you heard from them?"

"Who?"

Nobody knew Mr. Simms had been the Tribe's elder statesman but me. I had kept his secret, which meant he kept his job.

"You know who."

Simms scanned the hall to make sure we were alone.

"They could be anywhere by now," he said, shaking his head. "Hopefully far away from here."

"But they must've told you *something*."

"I told them not to."

"Why?"

"Because I knew you'd come for me and try to find out."

I couldn't help but wince. "You're protecting them *from me*?"

Mr. Simms reached into his pocket. "I did get this. . . ."

A postcard.

There was nothing written on the back, save for the school's address, care of Mr. Simms. It could have been from anybody.

But I knew who. "It's Sully, isn't it?"

"Your guess is as good as mine," Simms shrugged.

I flipped it over and found a faded photograph of a lake on the front. A crew-cutted kid straight out of the nineteen sixties was squatting in a canoe, waving at the camera.

At the top, it read:

GREETINGS FROM LAKE WENDIGO!

Sellars and Cassidy stepped up behind Simms, looking none too happy.

"Officers!" I beamed, stuffing the postcard into my back pocket. "So glad you could make it."

"You gonna come peacefully this time," Cassidy asked, "or are we gonna have to use handcuffs?"

"Don't you two ever get tired of this routine? Don't you ever imagine there's more to life than this cat-and-mousing we find ourselves locked in, day after day?"

"Not again, kid," Sellars sighed. "Either do as we tell you, or we use force."

"I love it when you go all authoritarian, Officer Sellars. . . ."

"Count of three, Pendleton," Cassidy intoned. *"One."*

I turned to Mr. Simms. "What period are we in?"

"Third."

"Two."

"That means you just mopped the halls in the cafeteria, didn't you?"

"Just finished," he said.

"Right on schedule." I nodded. "Good to see you, Mr. Simms."

"Three."

I plowed past Sellars and Cassidy.

"Come back here!" Cassidy shouted.

"But you haven't gotten a tour of the school yet," I called over my shoulder. "Follow me!"

Sellars and Cassidy were on my heels. Sellars was slowing down but Cassidy kept right on me.

"If you're feeling peckish," I called, entering the cafeteria, "might I recommend the mashed potatoes and a dash of pepper spray. Simply divine!"

The floor shone like a fresh ice-skating rink. If I had the time to stop, I could have marveled at my own reflection.

Cassidy was only a few steps behind. Just when he reached out to grab my shoulder, I dropped into a perfect slider. By the time Cassidy caught on, he was already heading on a crash course for the hot-food steam tables.

"Whoa, whoa, whoa—" Cassidy skidded his heels into the linoleum, only to slip. Arms flailing, he tried to correct his balance as best he could, flinging one foot into the air as if he were a lumbering figure skater performing a camel spin.

Cassidy made impact with the steam table—*THWACK*—sending a hailstorm of chicken nuggets into the air and showering back down upon him.

"Whenever you're ready for round two, just let me know," I said, picking up a nugget and taking a bite. "No rush. Take your time. Rest a sec."

Cassidy rolled over the floor, covered in nuggets, moaning low.

I held out my inhaler to him. "Here. Let me freshen you up."

Sellars ran into the cafeteria, hyperventilating, blocking my exit.

So this was where I'd take my last stand.

Showdown at the OK Cafeteria.

I clambered behind the steam tables, quickly presented with a vast array of dining choices.

What do we have on the menu today?

From the looks of it, we had a wide selection of foods to choose from—green peas and cubed carrots, baked beans with bacon bits drifting in bubbling brown sauce, a washed-out fruit salad, mac n' cheese, along with our aforementioned arsenal of chicken nuggets—each sitting in its own stainless steel heating tray.

A plastic-handled serving scoop pierced the surface of each grub tub.

I grabbed for the nearest ladle and served Sellars a hearty dollop of baked beans, splattered across the front of his uniform.

I seized a second scoop, double-fisting now, brandishing both like a pair of six shooters.

"Make sure you get a bit of all four food groups," I shouted as I fired off a scoop of mac n' cheese with my left hand, and peas with my right.

I'd become a culinary quick-draw.

Cassidy clamored up from the floor just in time to receive a face full of fruit salad. I was rapid-firing now, ladling up and hurling away.

"Eat melon balls, coppers!"

Both officers shielded their faces and stormed the steam tables.

That left the kitchen. I rushed into the back area, quickly met by a posse of hairnetted lunch ladies prepping for today's meal.

"Surprise health inspection!" I shouted before bolting for the storage freezer.

A bean-battered Sellars took the left while a mac-n'-cheesed Cassidy took the right, cornering me and closing in.

I tried sidestepping them, but they pounced before I could push through.

"I'm getting really tired of your routine, kid," Sellars said as he dragged me out of the kitchen, my heels squealing over the linoleum.

"That's what I've been saying all this time! But what else am I supposed to do with myself, locked up all day? The only way I can get you guys to come visit is when I break out from house arrest."

"Try and get some friends your own age."

Mr. Simms had entered the cafeteria, wheeling in his mop and bucket.

"My friends broke out a long time ago," I said. "I'm trying to find them."

"If you do, tell them I said hello," Simms said.

I could tell he missed them.

He wasn't the only one.